AF254769

CYNTHIA HICKEY

He's Coming for You

The Sheriff of Misty Hollow, Book 9

By Cynthia Hickey

ISBN-13:978-1-968792-96-1

Prologue

Ten Years Ago

The room smelled faintly of coffee and old paper. Sheriff Shea Callahan sat across from the man who had buried his wife.

At least, that's what every instinct in her body told her.

He didn't look like a killer.

That was the problem.

Clean-cut. Well-dressed. Hands folded neatly on the metal table as if he waited for a business meeting instead of an interrogation. No twitch. No sweat. No cracks. Just… calm. Too calm.

"Mr. Morrison." Shea slid a file onto the table between them. "Your wife didn't fall."

His eyes flicked briefly to the file, then back to her.

"I've already told you what happened."

"Yes," she said. "You have." That didn't mean he told the truth.

Jennifer Morrison had been found at the base of a rocky overlook just outside town. Broken bones. Blunt force trauma. The kind of injuries that came from a fall—unless you knew what to look for.

Unless you knew the difference between falling…and being pushed.

"You said she slipped," Shea continued. "Lost her footing near the edge."

"That's right."

"And yet." She tapped the file, "There are finger-shaped bruises on her upper arms."

Silence stretched between them. Not defensive. Not nervous. Measured.

He tilted his head slightly. "My wife was upset. I tried to steady her. That's hardly unusual. I would have to grip her hard to keep her from falling."

"She was afraid of you."

That landed.

Not visibly—but Shea felt it. A shift, subtle as a shadow passing over glass.

"She was *emotional*," he corrected. "We were having marital difficulties. I'm sure you understand how that can look… from the outside. I love my wife, Detective. Very much."

Shea didn't respond. Instead, she opened the file and turned it toward him. Photos.

Jennifer's arms. The bruises. The angle. The pressure points. Evidence that said *someone had held on… and not to help.* "You were the last person to see her alive."

"Yes."

"You argued."

"Yes."

"You grabbed her."

"I tried to stop her from leaving."

"And then she went over the edge."

He held her gaze. Unblinking. "That's what happened." The words were smooth. Practiced. Rehearsed.

Shea leaned back slightly in her chair, studying him. Ten years on the job had taught her one thing above all else: Guilty people lied.

But the dangerous ones? They believed their own version of the truth.

"You're very controlled," she said.

A faint smile touched his lips. Not warm. Not kind. Just… aware. "Is that a crime?"

"Not by itself."

Another stretch of silence.

He didn't fidget. Didn't look away. Didn't fill the space. He let her sit in it.

Confident. Comfortable. Like a man who knew exactly how this would end.

Shea closed the file. "You loved her?" she asked.

"Of course."

"But she filed reports," Shea said. "Spoke to a social worker. Told people she was afraid. She was seeing a psychiatrist."

His expression didn't change. "People say a lot of things when they're upset."

"She was planning to leave you."

A pause. Then, softly: "Everyone says that."

Something cold slid down Shea's spine. Not the words. The tone.

Detached. Observant.

Like he wasn't talking about his wife—but about people in general.

"She didn't fall." Shea leaned forward. Close enough that her voice didn't need to rise. "You pushed her."

There it was. The moment. The place where most suspects cracked, snapped, or scrambled to defend themselves.

He didn't. He just watched her. Studied her. Really *looked* at her for the first time.

And then—he smiled. It wasn't wide. It wasn't dramatic. It was small and private. Almost… impressed. "You're very certain."

"I am."

Another pause. Then he leaned forward too, mirroring her posture. Lowering his voice to match hers. "So am I."

The air in the room shifted.

Shea held his gaze, refusing to break first. Behind

the calm, behind the control, she could feel it now—Something coiled. Patient. Waiting.

"You won't be able to prove it," he said.

Not a threat.

A statement.

And that, more than anything, made her pulse kick.

Because he wasn't hoping.

He *knew*.

She straightened slowly, masking the flicker of anger. "We'll see about that."

He leaned back again, hands folding neatly once more. "Detective," he said, almost conversationally, "you seem like someone who doesn't like loose ends."

"I don't."

Another small smile. "I'll remember that." Something in the way he said it made the words linger. "I'm the same way."

Not in the room—but under her skin.

An officer knocked lightly on the door and stepped in. "Ma'am, the lawyer's here."

Of course he was. Right on time.

Shea stood, gathering the file. But before she turned away, she met his eyes one last time. "I know what you did," she said quietly.

For just a fraction of a second, something sharpened in his gaze. Not fear or guilt. Recognition.

Then it was gone. Replaced by that same calm, controlled expression. "Then I suppose," he said, "you'll have to live with that."

Shea turned and marched out. But the feeling followed her.

That she had just stepped into something—not finished…not resolved…just waiting.

Chapter One

Shea didn't answer right away. Her stomach dropped like a stone, and she plopped into a kitchen chair.

For one suspended second, she stood there in the middle of her kitchen with the phone pressed to her ear, every muscle in her body gone rigid. Trevor sat at the table, his expression sharpening as he watched her face drain of color.

The voice on the line was silent now. Waiting.

Shea forced herself to breathe. "Who is this?"

A soft crackle hummed over the connection. Then the same voice, flattened and scrubbed clean of any identifying edge. "Did you really think he worked alone?"

The kitchen seemed to shrink around her.

Trevor got out of his chair and took one step forward. "What is it?"

She lifted a hand to silence him, eyes fixed on nothing. "If you've got something to say, say it."

A pause. Then a faint sound reached her through the line. At first, she thought it was static. Then she realized it was something else.

Music. Tinny and distant. Like a child's music box winding down.

She strained to hear it.

The voice came back, low and deliberate. "You missed once. Will it happen again?"

A chill slid through her chest.

"Who is this?" she snapped.

No answer.

Just a click.

The line went dead.

She jerked the phone away from her ear and stared at the blank screen as if she could force it to reveal the man on the other end.

"Shea?" Trevor was beside her now, close enough that she could feel the tension coming off him. "What did he say?"

She swallowed, but her throat had gone dry. "He said, 'Did you really think he worked alone?'"

Trevor's jaw tightened.

She replayed the second sentence in her mind. *You missed once.*

Not *Pritchard.*

Trevor reached for the phone. "Let me see it."

She handed it over. His thumb moved quickly over the screen while she tried to slow the pounding in her chest. Outside, the town had settled into the fragile quiet that came after midnight. The kind of silence that never lasted long in Misty Hollow.

Trevor cursed under his breath. "Blocked number."

"Of course it was."

He looked up. "Could be somebody screwing with you. News of Pritchard's arrest is everywhere by now."

"No." The word came out too fast. Too certain.

Trevor studied her. "You know that already?"

She wrapped her arms around herself, though she wasn't cold. "He knew too much."

"About what?"

But she already knew. Or maybe she didn't know so much as feel it moving toward her, a shape just beyond the reach of logic.

You missed once.

Her mind flashed backward ten years with brutal clarity. A gray interview room. Metal table. Calm hands folded like a churchgoer's. Eyes that never once dropped under pressure.

You won't be able to prove it.

Jennifer Morrison's husband. The man who had walked. The man Shea had never been able to forget.

Trevor saw it happen on her face. "Who are you thinking of?"

She hesitated only a moment. "Jennifer Morrison's husband."

His expression changed. "From the old overlook case?"

She nodded.

"The wife murder."

"She didn't fall," Shea said quietly. "She was pushed."

Trevor exhaled slowly. He'd heard that story before, but only in fragments. Pieces dropped late at night over coffee, when one case bled into another and old failures surfaced like bodies in deep water. "You think this call has something to do with him?"

"I think somebody wanted me to think about him." Maybe Morrison himself.

Trevor handed the phone back. "That's not the same thing."

"No." Shea glanced at the dark window over the sink. Her reflection hovered there, pale and tense. "But it's close enough."

The kitchen still smelled faintly of coffee from hours earlier. Her jacket hung over the back of a chair. A case file sat open on the table, notes from Pritchard's interviews scattered beside it. An hour ago, she'd let herself believe it was over. That whatever horror he'd set in motion had finally burned out. Now it felt like she'd only been looking at the front door while someone else stood at the back.

Trevor picked up the file and flipped through the top pages. "Pritchard never gave us another name."

"No."

"Never hinted at a partner."

"No."

"He barely held together by the time we took him

in."

Shea turned, irritation flaring. Not at Trevor, but at the sick certainty growing inside her. "Because he wasn't the one steering it."

Trevor closed the file. "That's a leap."

"Is it?" She stepped toward the table and jabbed a finger at the papers. "Pritchard was unstable, sick, medicated half the time, and obsessed with symbolism. But some of the victim connections were too clean. Too organized. He shouldn't have known all of it. Not that well."

Trevor was quiet for a beat. "You think somebody fed him targets."

"I think somebody used him. Yes." The words fell between them like a door slamming shut.

Trevor ran a hand over his jaw. "Then why call you now?"

Because this wasn't over. Because the point of the call wasn't information. It was theater. Because whoever had called wanted her awake in the middle of the night, thinking about unfinished business and ghosts she'd failed to bury.

She didn't say any of that aloud. Instead, she said, "To make sure I know."

A sound cut through the room before Trevor could answer.

Three sharp knocks.

Not at the front door. At the back.

Both of them froze.

Trevor's hand went automatically to his sidearm. Shea felt every nerve in her body come alive at once with the burning surge of adrenaline. The knock came again, firm and deliberate.

Someone who expected the door to open.

Trevor moved first, crossing the kitchen in two silent steps and shifting to the side of the frame. Shea grabbed her own weapon from the counter where she'd set it down earlier and flattened herself against the wall opposite him.

Another knock.

Trevor mouthed, "Call it in."

She gave one tight nod and reached for her radio with her free hand, whispering their location and requesting backup. By the time dispatch confirmed units en route, the knocking had stopped. The silence that followed was worse.

Trevor leaned closer to the window in the door without exposing himself. "I don't see anyone."

Shea's pulse hammered. "Could be a trap."

"Probably is." He eased the door open just enough to check the porch, then wider. Cold night air spilled into the kitchen. The porch light cast a weak yellow circle over the back steps and the patch of yard beyond. Empty.

No movement. No car engine fading into the distance. No footsteps. Nothing.

Trevor swept the porch and yard with his light while Shea held position in the doorway. The woods beyond the property line stood black and still.

Then she saw it. "Trevor."

He followed her gaze downward.

Something sat in the center of the back doormat. A small object.

He crouched slowly, gun still angled low and stared at it for a second before picking it up with two fingers.

"What is that?" Shea asked.

He straightened and brought it under the kitchen light.

An old metal shoe buckle. Dull silver. Tarnished with age.

For a moment, neither of them spoke. Then Trevor said, "Does this mean something to you?"

Shea looked at the buckle and felt the room tilt very slightly. Not because she understood it.

Because she didn't. Not yet.

But she knew instinctively it wasn't random. Nothing about tonight was random.

Trevor set it carefully on the table and pulled a handkerchief from his pocket to avoid smudging it. "Could be from a costume. Could be junk somebody found in an antique shop."

"Could be a message."

His eyes met hers. "About what?"

She stared at the buckle. Something about its shape tugged at the edge of memory, but the connection wouldn't form. Instead, another detail from the call surfaced.

The faint music. Not a music box. Not exactly.

A voice, maybe. Children's voices.

Singing.

Her stomach tightened. "Trevor…"

He waited.

"I think I heard a nursery rhyme."

That got his attention. "On the call?"

She nodded slowly. "Very faint. Like it was in the background."

"Are you sure?"

"No." She hated the uncertainty in her own voice. "But I think so."

Trevor glanced back toward the open door, then shut it and locked it firmly before returning to the table. "Okay. Then we treat all of this as real."

She almost laughed at that, though nothing about the moment was funny. "You say that like we have a choice."

Headlights swept briefly across the front of the house. Backup arriving.

Trevor moved toward the living room to meet them, but Shea stayed where she was and stared at the buckle lying on the wood grain of her table like a clue dropped from another lifetime.

You missed once.

She thought of Jennifer Morrison again. Her blonde hair darkened by dirt and blood at the bottom of the overlook, bruises on her arms, fear documented too late. She thought of her husband sitting in that interview room, so controlled, so sure of himself, as if he were already standing in the future looking back at her failure.

And now this. A phone call in the middle of the night. A disguised male voice. A warning.

Trevor returned with two deputies, and the kitchen filled with movement—questions, photographs, gloves, the scrape of chairs. Shea answered what she had to, but her mind remained fixed on the same point. Someone had reached through the thin layer of peace left after Pritchard's arrest and torn it wide open.

Deputy Butler photographed the buckle, then looked up. "You want it bagged and sent to the lab?"

"Yes." Shea nodded.

Trevor was already on his phone, contacting the state tech unit to see whether anything could be pulled from the blocked call, though they both knew the odds were slim.

Butler slipped the buckle into an evidence bag. As he sealed it, he frowned. "This sounds strange, but… was there anything else left out here?"

"What do you mean?" Shea asked.

He hesitated. "There's a mark on the porch rail. Like something scratched into the paint."

Shea crossed the room in three strides. Trevor followed.

Under the porch light, on the flat top of the rail beside the door, a shape had been carved into the white paint. Not deep, but deliberate. Done with something sharp.

A number.

1

Nothing else. Just that single, neat digit.

Shea stared at it, every beat of her heart suddenly loud in her ears.

Trevor looked at her. "You know what it means?"

A cold certainty moved through her, settling bone-deep. Not fully understood.

The buckle. The nursery rhyme. The number one. And a voice asking if she really thought Pritchard had worked alone.

She lifted her gaze to the darkness beyond the yard, to the tree line where anything could be hiding and often was. "No," she said. "But I think we're about to find out."

She didn't sleep that night.

By dawn, Misty Hollow was washed in pale gray light and low mountain fog often associated with early Spring. The buckle was on its way to the lab. The porch rail had been photographed, cast, and measured. The call trace had yielded nothing useful. Shea sat in her office with a fresh cup of coffee gone cold beside her, Jennifer Morrison's old file open in front of her for the first time in years.

She had no business reopening it based on one phone call and a piece of metal left on her porch. She knew that. But her gut had carried her through too many bad nights to ignore it now.

Trevor entered without knocking, holding a thin paper sack from the bakery and two more coffees. He set one on her desk and glanced at the open file. "So, we're doing this."

She looked up at him. "You can tell me I'm wrong."

"I could," he said. "But I don't think you'd listen."

A tired smile almost touched her mouth, but didn't quite make it. "Probably not."

After giving her a quick kiss, he pulled out the chair across from her and sat. "I made a few calls on Morrison before coming in."

That sharpened her attention. "And?"

"He still lives two counties over. Same name. Same clean record since acquittal. Taxes paid on time. No arrests. No obvious reason to pop back onto our radar."

"Men like him don't need obvious reasons."

Trevor slid a printout across the desk. "Maybe not. But there's more."

She took it. A recent photo. DMV renewal. Older now, a little heavier through the face, but still with that same composed expression. That same maddening impression of order. Of control.

Shea's jaw tightened.

Trevor watched her. "You know what bothers me?"

"Only one thing?"

He ignored that. "If this was him, why call? Why leave a clue? Why not just disappear into the dark and do whatever he's planning?"

Because men like him didn't just want to win. They wanted to be known for winning.

They wanted witnesses. They wanted an audience.

Before she could answer, the phone on her desk rang. The sound sliced through the room.

Both of them stared at it. Not her cell this time.

The office line.

Shea picked it up on the second ring. "Sheriff Callahan."

For a heartbeat, there was only breathing. Then a woman's voice, shaky and thin with terror. "I think he's here."

Shea straightened. "Who is this?"

"Lila Vance." A ragged inhale. "I served on that jury ten years ago. The Morrison trial."

Every muscle in Shea's body locked.

Trevor had gone still across from her, reading the change in her face.

"Ms. Vance, listen to me carefully. Are you alone?"

"I saw someone in the pasture." Her voice broke. "There's black wool tied to my fence."

Shea was already on her feet.

Trevor stood with her.

"Lock your doors." Shea grabbed her keys. "Do not go outside. We're on our way."

The line crackled. In the background, faint and distant, Shea heard something she wished she hadn't recognized.

A man's voice. Softly singing. "Baa, baa, black sheep…"

Then Lila screamed.

And the line went dead.

Chapter Two

The tires crunched over gravel as Trevor turned onto the narrow drive. The cruiser's headlights cut through the low fog that had settled across the pasture. Morning had begun to press faint light into the sky, but it hadn't reached the ground yet, leaving everything washed in gray shadow.

Shea leaned forward slightly in her seat, her attention fixed ahead. "Unit already on scene?" she asked.

Trevor nodded. "First deputy got here a few minutes ago. Said the caller stopped responding."

That didn't sit right. Calls dropped. People panicked. But there was a difference between a broken connection and a voice that simply... stopped. Then, a scream.

As the drive curved, the farmhouse came into view. A porch light glowed weakly against the lingering darkness, and a patrol vehicle sat near the front with its engine still running. No lights flashed. No one moved outside.

The quiet pressed in.

Trevor slowed the cruiser. "We go in careful."

"Agreed."

They stepped out into the chilly Spring air together. Colder than it should have been in March, it bit through Shea's jacket as her boots hit the gravel. Her focus moved automatically across the property—house, yard, tree line—until it caught on something along the fence.

A dark shape. Still. Wrong.

Her pulse kicked, but she kept her movements controlled as they approached the porch.

Deputy Butler stepped out to meet them, his expression already tight with unease. "She called it in," he said quietly. "Said she saw something out in the pasture. Then the line went dead."

"I spoke with her. She inside?" Shea asked.

Butler hesitated. "No. We cleared the house. She's not there." The answer settled heavily between them.

Trevor glanced past the deputy toward the yard, then back to Shea. "Let's take a look."

They moved through the gate and into the pasture. The damp grass soaked into their boots as they crossed the open ground. With each step, the shape on the fence became clearer, resolving into something that made Shea's chest tighten.

By the time they reached it, there was no question.

Lila Vance's body had been draped over the top

rail of the fence. Her arms hung loosely on one side, fingers brushing the grass, while her head tilted at an unnatural angle. Her hair clung darkly to her face, where it had dried with blood.

What drew Shea's attention first, though, was the wool. Thick black wool had been laid across Lila's shoulders and back, heavy and out of place against the pale morning. It hadn't come from the pasture. It had been brought here.

Three small sacks hung from the fence beside her, tied in a neat row. Each one bore a label written in careful, deliberate lettering.

Shea stepped closer and read them silently. "Master. Dame. Little Boy."

Trevor let out a slow breath behind her. "That's not subtle."

"No." Shea exhaled heavily. "It's not meant to be."

She crouched and studied the ground near the fence. The grass showed signs of disturbance. Flattened in places, scuffed in others, but the marks were contained. There had been movement here, but not chaos. No wide struggle, no frantic attempt to escape. Whoever had done this had controlled the moment.

"She didn't get far." Trevor followed her gaze.

"No," Shea agreed. "Either he kept her off balance… or she never had the chance."

Butler shifted behind them. "We didn't find anything in the house. No sign of forced entry. No blood inside."

"She came out on her own," Trevor said.

"Or she was made to believe she needed to." Shea straightened. Her eyes moved over the scene again, taking in the placement of the body, the wool, the sacks. Everything had been arranged with intention. Nothing about it was rushed.

Her gaze settled on the fence post.

A mark had been carved into the wood just beside where Lila's body hung. The paint had been scratched away in a clean, deliberate line.

The number **1**.

A cold recognition moved through her.

Trevor saw it a moment later. "Same as your porch."

"Yes."

He exhaled slowly. "So, this is the beginning of another game."

She didn't answer. She didn't need to. They both knew the answer was yes.

Behind them, the sound of another vehicle approaching broke through the stillness. Shea glanced toward the drive as two figures stepped out of a dark SUV.

Agents Snelling and Webster moved toward them, their expressions tightening as they took in the scene. Snelling stopped a few feet away, her gaze sweeping over the body, the wool, the sacks. "You've got to be kidding me. Is this town ever peaceful?"

Webster crouched slightly, careful not to cross any

of the emerging evidence markers. "This is cleaner than Pritchard," he said after a moment. "More controlled."

"It is," Shea said. "And more deliberate."

Snelling looked at her. "You got that call last night."

She nodded. "Yes."

"And now this."

"Yes."

Webster straightened, brushing his hands together as she stood. "You still think there's another person involved."

"I think this is the person who was always involved," Shea said.

Snelling's jaw tightened. "That's a serious claim."

"So is this." Shea gestured toward the body.

Trevor stepped closer, his voice low. "We've got the same marking. Number one."

Webster's attention sharpened. "Number one?"

Shea nodded. "It was carved into my porch rail last night."

Snelling's gaze snapped to her. "Your house?"

"Yes."

"Why wasn't that reported immediately?"

"It was documented," Trevor said evenly. "We just didn't have a body to go with it."

Now they did.

Webster looked back at the sacks, then at the wool. "Baa, Baa, Black Sheep," he said.

The words settled into place.

Shea felt it click—not as a surprise, but as a confirmation. "Yes."

Snelling shook his head slightly. "So, we're looking at what, someone staging murders around nursery rhymes? Like he did with the alphabet?"

Shea met her gaze. "We're looking at someone using them to communicate."

"To who?"

She didn't hesitate. "To me." Again. The implication lingered.

The wind moved faintly across the pasture, shifting the wool slightly where it lay across Lila's back. The motion was small, but it drew Shea's attention again to the deliberate nature of the scene.

This hadn't been left behind carelessly. It had been presented.

~

From the edge of the trees, he watched the scene unfold.

He had chosen the position carefully. Far enough back to remain unseen, close enough to observe without obstruction. The early morning fog helped, softening the edges of movement, blending shadow and distance into something difficult to read.

The sheriff moved through the scene with a kind of control he appreciated. She did not rush, did not react outwardly in ways that distracted her from what mattered. Instead, she studied the details, allowing them to settle into place before drawing conclusions.

That was why she had been a problem before. And why she would be again.

He watched as she noticed the wool, then the sacks, then the marking on the fence. Each step of recognition came in the correct order. There was no hesitation, no misinterpretation.

She understood the structure. Not fully. Not yet. But enough. That was important.

The others followed her lead. The deputy stayed just behind her, attentive, protective, but waiting. The federal agents observed with a mixture of skepticism and interest, their confidence shifting as the scene revealed itself.

They were catching up.

But she was already there.

His gaze drifted briefly to the body.

Lila Vance had been necessary only because of what she represented. A voice in a room that had reached the wrong conclusion. A piece of a process that had failed.

He did not think of her beyond that.

The act itself had been efficient, controlled, exactly as intended. There had been a moment, brief and fleeting, when she had understood what was happening. He had seen it in her eyes.

Fear, then recognition. Then nothing.

His attention returned to the sheriff as she spoke to the others, explaining, interpreting, guiding the understanding of the scene.

She was already stepping into the role he needed her to occupy.

Not just an investigator, but a participant.

He allowed himself a small, private smile.

It had begun.

~

The medical examiner arrived half an hour later. Evidence markers appeared in the grass. Photographs were taken from multiple angles. Gloves snapped into place as the process shifted from discovery to documentation.

Shea stepped back, giving the team room to work, but she didn't take her eyes off the fence.

Trevor moved beside her. "You okay?"

"I'm fine."

"You don't look fine."

She let out a quiet breath. "He called me last night."

"I know."

"And now this."

Trevor nodded. "You think he was already here when he called." It wasn't a question.

"Yes.".

Trevor glanced toward the tree line. "Then he could still be close."

"Or he wanted us to think that."

Trevor's jaw tightened. "Either way, we expand the perimeter."

Snelling was already giving that order, deputies

moving outward to search the surrounding area.

Webster approached Shea again, his expression thoughtful. "You said you heard something on the call."

Shea nodded. "Music. Or singing."

"What kind?"

Shea closed her eyes briefly, replaying the memory. It was faint, almost lost in the background, but now that she focused on it, it felt clearer.

"Children's voices," she said. "Or something meant to sound like them."

Webster's gaze shifted back to the body. "Nursery rhymes."

"Yes."

Snelling looked between them. "We've got a second offender, organized, deliberate, using symbolism tied to childhood songs and targeting people connected to a past case."

Shea met his gaze. "Not just any case."

"The Morrison case," Trevor said.

Snelling exhaled slowly. "Ten years ago."

"Yes."

"And you think this is tied to that husband."

"I think," Shea said carefully, "that he's been waiting."

"For what?" Webster asked.

Shea looked back at the number carved into the fence. "For the right moment." Neither Shea or Morrison liked things left incomplete.

Her phone vibrated in her pocket. The sensation

was sharp enough to immediately draw her attention. She pulled it out and glanced at the screen.

Unknown number.

Trevor saw it. "Don't—"

She answered anyway. "This is Sheriff Callahan."

For a moment, there was only silence. Then, the same controlled breathing. "You see it now."

Shea turned slightly, scanning the pasture, the tree line, the open space beyond the fence. "You're watching."

A pause. "I'm observing."

Her grip tightened on the phone. "You killed her."

"I corrected a mistake."

The words were calm, measured, as if he were explaining something simple.

"She served on a jury during your trial," Shea said. "That's not a mistake."

"It was."

Her jaw tightened. "You don't get to decide that."

"I already have."

She forced herself to stay steady. "Why the number?"

Another pause. Then, quietly: "You'll understand soon enough."

The line went dead. She lowered the phone slowly as her hand shook.

Trevor was watching her closely. "What did he say?"

She didn't take her eyes off the fence. "He said this

is about correcting a mistake."

Snelling swore under her breath.

Webster's voice was quieter. "And the number?"

Shea's gaze remained fixed on the carved **1**. "He said I'll understand." This was, without a doubt, Morrison behind it all.

The wind shifted again, moving faintly through the pasture. For just a moment, Shea thought she heard something carried with it. The faint echo of a melody she couldn't quite place.

Not real. Not here. Just memory. Or something meant to feel like it.

She turned to look out toward the trees, the fog still lingering between them.

Nothing moved. Nothing revealed itself. But the certainty settled deeper.

This wasn't random, and it was just beginning. And whatever came next had already been planned.

She looked back at the scene, at the structure of it, at the message that had been left for her to find and spoke her thoughts out loud. "This is just the beginning."

No one argued.

Because they all knew it was true.

Chapter Three

By the time Shea returned to the station, the morning had settled into a deceptive normal.

Sunlight stretched across Main Street, catching on storefront windows and the steady movement of people beginning their day. A delivery truck idled near Lucy's Café. Someone laughed outside the hardware store. Life continued, unbothered. It always did.

Shea pushed through the front doors of the sheriff's office, the familiar hum of activity greeting her. Radios crackled. Phones rang. Deputies moved through the space with quiet efficiency.

Trevor was already inside, standing near the bullpen with a file tucked under one arm and a cup of coffee in his hand. He looked up as she approached.

"ME confirmed time of death," he said without preamble. "Between two and three."

"That tracks," Shea replied. "She called just before that."

Trevor nodded. "Single blow, maybe two. Nothing

messy."

"Nothing messy," Shea echoed.

That detail lingered. It fit too well with what she had seen…and what she had begun to suspect.

Before she could say more, a voice cut in from behind them.

"Sheriff Callahan."

Shea turned.

Agent Snelling stood a few steps away, composed and observant, her dark hair pulled back neatly. Beside her, Agent Webster gave a brief nod, his posture relaxed but his attention sharp.

"Agents," Shea said. "Let's talk." She waved them into the conference room.

~

Photos from the pasture scene were spread across the table. Lila Vance draped over the fence, the wool, the labeled sacks. Even in still images, the deliberate nature of the staging was unmistakable.

Snelling studied them for a moment before speaking. "This isn't consistent with Pritchard."

"No," Shea said. "It's not."

Webster crossed his arms. "Pritchard's scenes had structure, but they were unstable. This is controlled."

"Planned," Trevor added.

Shea nodded. "Whoever did this knew exactly what they were doing."

Snelling looked at her. "You believe there's another offender."

"I think there always was. Someone else running the whole thing."

Webster tilted his head slightly. "And you believe that person was directing Pritchard."

"Yes."

"Why wouldn't Pritchard say anything?" Webster asked.

"Because he didn't think he was being directed," Shea said. "He thought he was being helped or maybe he really did think he was the one in control."

Snelling's expression shifted, interest sharpening. "Meaning someone reframed his actions for him."

"Maybe. Yes," Shea said. "Someone gave him a purpose he could believe in."

The room fell quiet for a moment as that settled in.

Trevor broke it. "So now we've got someone more organized, more patient, and more deliberate picking up where Pritchard left off."

"Or continuing something that never stopped," Shea said.

Before anyone could respond, Trevor's radio crackled sharply.

"Unit three, respond to 214 Maple Street. Possible DOA. Female victim found seated at the kitchen table. Reporting party states the scene appears staged."

The room stilled.

Trevor looked at Shea.

She didn't hesitate. "Let's go."

Maple Street was quiet in the way neighborhoods

often were in the late morning—cars parked neatly in driveways, curtains half-drawn, neighbors watching from a distance without stepping too close.

A patrol unit sat at the curb, and a small group had already gathered across the street, their voices low and uncertain.

Shea stepped out of the cruiser, her senses sharpening as she took in the scene. Trevor joined her, and behind them, Snelling and Webster marched toward the house.

A uniformed deputy met them at the front door. "Sheriff."

"What do we have?" Shea asked.

"Neighbor found her when she didn't answer. Said she looked like she was just sitting there, but something wasn't right. They called it in right away."

"House clear?"

"Yes, ma'am."

Shea nodded. "Let's take a look."

The interior of the home was tidy, almost meticulously so. Nothing appeared disturbed in the living room. No signs of forced entry. No indication of a struggle.

It wasn't until they reached the kitchen that everything shifted.

Shea slowed in the doorway.

The victim sat at the small kitchen table, her posture upright, her hands resting loosely in her lap. At first glance, she might have been mistaken for someone lost in thought.

But the stillness was wrong. Absolute. Final.

In front of her sat a white ceramic bowl filled with cottage cheese. A spider floated in the center.

Trevor stopped just behind Shea, his voice low. "That's intentional."

"Yes." Shea pressed her lips together. Everything Morrison did was intentional.

Snelling stepped into the room, her gaze moving over the details. "No signs of disturbance," she observed. "Everything's in place."

"She either trusted him," Webster said, "or didn't realize what was happening until it was too late."

Shea moved closer, her attention fixed on the bowl. The spider was large, its dark body stark against the pale surface beneath it.

"This wasn't found here," she said.

Snelling nodded. "No. That's not a local species."

"So, it was brought in," Trevor said.

"Yes," Snelling replied. "Chosen. Have someone find out where this spider had been purchased."

Webster's gaze shifted to the victim's face. "Cause of death?"

"Prelim says likely poisoning," the deputy said from the doorway. "ME's on the way."

Shea stepped slightly to the side to take in the full scene again. The placement of the chair. The angle of the victim's head. The bowl sat positioned directly in front of her.

"Little Miss Muffet," she said.

Trevor nodded grimly. "Sat on a tuffet, eating her curds and whey."

"And along came a spider," Snelling finished.

Webster exhaled slowly. "Second in the sequence."

Shea's gaze shifted to the wall beside the doorway. There, carved cleanly into the paint just above the light switch, was the number **2**. Her chest tightened.

"He's marking them," Trevor said.

"And he's counting," Webster added.

Shea nodded. Two victims. Two scenes. Two messages.

And both had been left for her to find. The killer moved fast.

~

He had anticipated the timing with precision.

Morning discovery created a different kind of impact. It allowed the scene to settle in the quiet hours, undisturbed, before being introduced into the rhythm of the day. By the time it was found, it was no longer an event. It was a fact.

He had not stayed long after finishing. There was no reason to. The arrangement had been correct. The outcome assured. Still, he allowed himself the memory of it.

The way she had sat across from him, unaware of what was coming. The moment of confusion when the first symptoms set in. The brief flicker of realization that followed.

He did not dwell on it. The act itself was not the focus. The structure was.

Each element had been chosen carefully. The bowl. The contents. The spider. The positioning. Everything aligned with the message.

And the message mattered.

Because *she* would see it.

She would stand in that kitchen and recognize the pattern, just as she had recognized the first. She would begin to anticipate what came next.

That was the purpose. This was not meant to confuse her. It was meant to guide her.

He moved through the edges of the town without drawing attention, blending into the spaces between observation and absence. The morning continued around him, unaware.

It would not remain that way for long. It never did.

His thoughts returned, as they often did, to the same point. Not the victims. Not the sequence.

Her.

~

"She was the stenographer." Trevor scrolled through records on his phone. "Worked the Morrison trial like the first victim."

Shea nodded. "She recorded everything."

Webster looked at her. "Which means, in Morrison's mind, she preserved the version of events that let him go free."

"Yes."

Snelling stepped back from the table, her expression thoughtful. "We're looking at jurors, court staff… anyone who played a role in that outcome."

Trevor exhaled. "That's a long list."

"Not if he's narrowing it by function," Shea said. "He's not picking randomly. He's choosing positions."

Webster glanced at the carved number again. "Then this isn't just a pattern. It's a sequence with an endpoint."

Shea felt that settle. "Yes."

"And we don't know how many steps there are," Snelling added.

"No," Shea said. "But we can find out."

She turned toward Trevor. "Pull every record from that trial. Jurors, alternates, attorneys, clerks, witnesses. Everyone."

"I'm on it."

Snelling nodded. "We'll cross-reference with federal databases."

Webster added, "And we start protection protocols for anyone still alive on that list."

Shea looked back at the victim. At the bowl. At the spider. At the number carved into the wall.

"He's not just recreating the trial," she said quietly.

Snelling met her gaze. "What do you think he's doing?"

Shea didn't hesitate.

"He's rewriting it."

The words hung in the air. Because they all

understood what that meant.

And because somewhere out there, he moved two steps ahead of them.

Chapter Four

The call came just before dawn, when the world was quiet enough for everything to feel sharper. Shea had not gone home.

The idea had crossed her mind once, sometime after two, when the station had briefly fallen into that strange lull between exhaustion and momentum. But the moment had passed, replaced by the steady pull of the case. There were too many pieces in motion now, too many questions pressing forward, and something about leaving, even for a few hours, felt like stepping away at the wrong moment.

So, she stayed.

The conference room lights had been dimmed at some point, though no one remembered doing it. Coffee cups had collected along the table, half-finished and forgotten. Files lay open in uneven stacks, names and photographs pinned across the board in front of Shea.

She stood there now, arms folded, staring at the growing pattern of notes on the crime scene board.

Lila Vance — Jury Foreman

Evelyn Hart — Court Stenographer

Two lives reduced to positions. Two roles extracted from a moment ten years ago and dragged into the present with brutal precision.

Behind her, Trevor shifted in his chair. If she didn't go home, he didn't. Always there in case she needed him.

The quiet creak of wood cut through the silence. He had loosened his tie hours ago, his sleeves rolled up, fatigue visible in the lines around his eyes. Stubble from needing to shave darkened his jawline. But he was still focused. Still present.

"You're seeing something," he said.

Shea didn't turn right away. Her eyes remained on the board. "I'm trying to see what he sees."

Trevor leaned forward, resting his elbows on his knees. "And?"

She let out a slow breath. "He's not just choosing people connected to the trial," she said. "He's choosing them based on how they fit into it."

Snelling looked up from her laptop. "Hierarchy."

"Yes," Shea said. "Order. Function. The jury foreman leads. The stenographer records. Each one plays a part."

Webster shifted his weight against the table as his gaze moved between the names. "Which means this isn't random escalation."

"No," Shea said quietly. "It's structured."

That word seemed to settle into the room like something heavy. Structured meant planned. Structured meant intentional. Structured meant it wouldn't stop on its own. It was all meant for Shea to stop. Something she'd failed to do ten years ago.

Trevor stood and moved closer to the board. His hand hovered near the pinned photographs without touching them. "If he's working through the system, then we need to figure out what comes next before he does."

Shea almost responded. Almost said *before he gets there.*

But something stopped her. Because the truth felt closer to this: He already had.

The phone rang. The sound cut through the room so sharply that all four of them turned toward it at once. In that moment, it felt like something more than the simple ringing of a phone. It felt like the next move in a conversation none of them had agreed to, or wanted, to have.

Trevor took a step toward it, but Shea moved first. She picked up the receiver, her hand steady even as something cold settled beneath her ribs. "Sheriff Callahan."

For a moment, there was nothing. Then—measured breathing.

Her fingers tightened slightly around the phone. "You're early."

A pause. "No, I'm on time."

The voice was the same—flattened, neutral, stripped of identity. It carried no age, no accent, no urgency. It sounded like someone who had taken care to remove everything that might betray him. He knew that she knew who he was so why disguise his voice? Part of the game?

She turned slightly, her eyes drifting back to the board. "What do you want?"

"I want you to understand."

Her gaze fixed on Lila Vance's name. "I understand enough," she said. "You're targeting people from the Morrison trial." His trial.

"That's part of it."

Her jaw tightened. "Then explain the rest."

There was a longer pause this time. When he spoke again, there was something beneath the calm. Something deliberate and almost reflective. "There will be one every day."

The words settled into her chest with a weight that didn't move.

"Until you catch me." The line went dead.

Shea lowered the receiver slowly, the quiet that followed pressing in from all sides.

Trevor stepped closer. "What did he say?"

She didn't look at him. "He said there will be a death every day until I catch him."

No one spoke.

Snelling was the first to move, closing her laptop with a soft click. "Then we're not just dealing with escalation," she said. "We're dealing with a timeline."

Webster nodded. "And he just defined it."

Trevor exhaled sharply. "That's not pressure. That's control."

Shea finally turned to face them. "It's both."

Before anyone could respond, Trevor's radio crackled.

"Unit three. Possible homicide at Archer Street. Business location. The reporting officer states the victim is inside. Scene appears staged like the others."

The words seemed to hang in the air.

Trevor closed his eyes briefly. "That didn't take long."

No. It hadn't.

Shea grabbed her jacket. "Let's go."

The morning light had strengthened by the time they reached Archer Street, but it did little to soften what waited there. The shop sat between two quiet storefronts, its painted sign worn but well-kept: Misty Hollow Clock & Repair. The front windows reflected the pale sky, giving nothing away. But the patrol car parked at the curb, and the officer waiting just outside the door, told a different story.

Shea stepped out of the cruiser, the cool air hitting her face as she took in the scene. There was no crowd here yet. No onlookers gathering. Just a stillness that felt like it was holding its breath.

The officer straightened as they approached. "Sheriff."

"What do we have?" Shea asked.

"Shop owner. Found by a customer when the door was open. Said something felt off."

Shea glanced at the door. It stood slightly ajar. "Anyone else inside?"

"No, ma'am. We cleared it."

She nodded. "All right."

She pushed the door open and stepped inside. The sound met her immediately. Ticking.

Dozens of clocks filled the space. Wall clocks, standing clocks, small mechanisms lined along shelves…each one marking time at its own pace. The overlapping rhythm created a low, constant pulse that filled the air.

It wasn't loud. But it was everywhere.

Trevor stepped in behind her, his eyes sweeping the room. "That's unsettling."

Shea didn't respond. She already moved further inside.

They passed through the front of the shop, weaving between displays and workbenches, the ticking growing louder the farther they went.

The back room was smaller. More contained. And in the center of it—the victim.

Shea slowed. Not because she didn't expect it. But because the way he had been left demanded that she take her time.

The man stood against a tall grandfather clock, his back pressed to its polished wood. His arms hung at his sides, his body held upright in a way that made it clear he had not died that way.

His head tilted slightly forward, chin lowered, as if in quiet resignation. Blood had seeped through his shirt, dark and spreading from a wound she could now see just beneath his ribs.

The clock behind him stood silent. Its hands frozen at exactly twelve.

Shea stepped closer. Her eyes moved carefully over the scene.

Snelling crouched and studied the floor, the placement, and the angle of the body. "Minimal disturbance again. No signs of a prolonged struggle."

Webster moved to the side, his gaze shifting upward to the clock face. "He creates conditions where there isn't one."

Shea's attention dropped to the base of the clock. There. Carved into the wood. She stepped closer, her eyes narrowing as she read the words.

THE CLOCK STRUCK WRONG

A chill moved through her. "Hickory Dickory Dock."

Trevor nodded. "The mouse ran up the clock…"

"And the clock struck one," Snelling finished.

Webster glanced at the frozen hands. "But this one didn't."

"No," Shea said. Her gaze lifted again to the clock face.

Twelve. Not one. Not the rhyme. Something else.

"This isn't just the rhyme," she said. "It's a correction."

Trevor frowned. "Of what?"

She turned slightly, meeting his eyes. "Time."

The word settled heavily.

Webster's gaze sharpened. "He thinks something ran out."

"Yes."

Snelling stood slowly. "Justice."

Shea nodded. "He thinks it was wrong the first time."

The officer behind them spoke quietly. "Name's Harold Briggs. Owned the shop."

Trevor pulled up his phone and scrolled quickly. "Hold on…" He stopped, then looked up. "Yeah. He's in the file."

Shea didn't need to ask.

"Bailiff," Trevor said.

The word landed with weight.

Snelling exhaled slowly. "Another role."

Webster nodded. "Another piece of the system."

Shea looked at the body again. At the clock. At the message carved into the wood.

~

He had always appreciated precision. Time required it.

The clocks in the shop had been a complication at first. Too many variables. Too many moving parts. But once he understood the rhythm of the place. The owner's habits, the timing of his work—it became manageable.

He had come here before. Weeks ago. Long enough to ask questions without raising suspicion. Long enough to confirm what he needed to know.

Names. Connections.

The past had a way of revealing itself when approached correctly. People did not guard history the way they guarded the present. They spoke more freely. Especially when they believed it no longer mattered.

He had listened and observed. Learned.

And when the time came, he acted.

The man had not understood at first. There had been confusion, then recognition, then something closer to fear.

It had been brief. It always was.

Now the scene stood as it was meant to.

He considered the sheriff again. She would understand this one differently. The shift in meaning. The movement from pattern to intention.

That mattered.

Because understanding brought her closer. And closeness was the point.

~

Shea stepped back and kept her gaze locked on the clock. The ticking from the rest of the shop pressed in around her, filling the silence with an uneven rhythm that made it difficult to think clearly. Or maybe it made things clearer. "He's been here before."

Trevor looked at her. "What makes you say that?"

She gestured subtly around the room. "Nothing here feels rushed. Nothing feels unfamiliar. He knew the layout. The timing. The victim."

Snelling nodded. "Pre-planning."

Webster added, "Which means this didn't start yesterday."

"No," Shea said.

Trevor looked down at his phone again. "There's more."

She turned to him.

"Customer report," he said. "Briggs mentioned a guy coming in a couple of weeks ago. Asking questions."

"What kind of questions?" Snelling asked.

"About people," Trevor said. "Names. Trial-related."

The room seemed to tighten again. Shea felt it settle into place. "He was building this."

"Yes," Webster replied. "Long before the first body."

Trevor exhaled. "Then we're not chasing him."

Shea looked back at the clock. "No, we're trying to catch up."

The ticking continued around them and cut to the very core of her. For the first time since the call that morning, Shea felt something she hadn't allowed herself to feel yet. Not fear. Something closer to pressure.

Because the man on the phone had been right about one thing. There would be another. Tomorrow. And unless they moved faster than he did, there would be one after that.

She turned toward the others, her voice steady but firm. "We don't wait."

Trevor met her gaze. "No."

Snelling nodded. "We start moving now."

Webster added, "Because he already is."

Shea looked once more at the stopped clock. At the frozen hands. At the message carved beneath it.

Then she said, quietly: "Let's make sure he doesn't stay ahead."

But even as she said it, she knew.

He already was.

Chapter Five

Shea woke the next morning by jerking upright in bed. For a second, she didn't know why.

Her pulse raced, her breath too quick, her body reacting before her mind could catch up. The room was dim with early morning light, the edges of the curtains glowing faintly as the sun began to rise.

From the other side of the bed, Heidi let out a low whine.

Shea turned her head, her hand automatically reaching over to rest against the German Shepherd's neck. Heidi leaned into the touch, steady and warm, but she hadn't barked. Hadn't moved toward the door. Hadn't given any sign that something was wrong outside.

Which meant whatever had pulled Shea out of sleep wasn't real. Not yet.

She let out a slow breath, forcing her shoulders to relax. "You're okay," she murmured, more to herself than to the dog.

Shea had fully expected to wake to the sound of her phone ringing. Another call, another body, another piece of the sequence falling into place exactly as the man had promised.

There will be one every day.

The words had followed her into sleep and lingered there, just beneath the surface. But the phone sat silent on her nightstand. For now.

She swung her legs over the side of the bed and sat there for a moment, elbows resting on her knees, her hands running through her hair as she tried to clear the fog from her mind.

Her body felt the exhaustion now that she had stopped moving. Hours of tension caught up all at once. But her mind refused to slow down.

She pushed herself to her feet. Would she actually get a quiet morning?

Breakfast. Coffee. A few minutes where nothing happened? The thought felt almost foreign.

Not trusting it, she padded down the hallway and into the kitchen. Heidi followed close behind, her nails clicking softly against the wood floor.

Shea opened the back door, letting the cool morning air spill into the room. "Go on."

Heidi stepped outside, nose already lowering to the ground as she moved into the yard.

Shea turned back to the counter and started the coffee pot. The machine hummed softly as it worked, filling the kitchen with the faint smell of brewing coffee.

For a moment, she just stood there, listening. No phone. No radio. No urgency. Just quiet.

She stepped out onto the back deck and leaned against the railing as she looked out over the woods beyond her property. Morning light filtered through the trees, catching on the leaves and shifting with the breeze.

It was peaceful. Convincingly so.

But Shea had lived in Misty Hollow long enough to know that peace and danger could exist side by side without warning. Trouble had come to this town before. And it had a way of staying.

The coffee pot dinged behind her, pulling her back inside. She poured herself a cup, black, and stepped back out onto the deck. Heidi moved through the yard, her posture relaxed, her tail low but steady as she explored familiar ground.

No tension. No alert.

For the first time in two days, Shea felt something loosen slightly in her chest. Until her phone rang.

The sound cut through the quiet like a blade. She froze. The cup hovered halfway to her lips, forgotten.

For a second, she didn't move. Didn't want to. Because she already knew what waited on the other end. He had told her. One every day. Her phone rang again.

She set the cup down slowly on the railing, the ceramic clicking faintly against the wood. Then she reached into her pocket and pulled the phone free.

Unknown number.

Her grip tightened. She answered. "This is Sheriff Callahan."

For a moment, there was nothing. Then—the breathing.

She turned slightly. Her eyes scanned the tree line beyond her yard, though she knew she wouldn't see anything. "You said one a day. That hasn't happened yet."

"Not yet."

Her fingers tightened around the phone. "Then why call?"

Another pause. When he spoke again, his voice carried that same calm certainty. "Because you're thinking in the wrong direction."

Her pulse kicked. "What does that mean?"

"You're waiting for me to act," he said. "But I already have."

The words settled cold in her chest. "Where?"

A faint shift in his breathing. Almost… satisfied. "Look closer." The line went dead.

Shea lowered the phone slowly, her mind already moving.

I already have.

Her gaze snapped back to the yard. Heidi had stopped moving.

The dog stood near the far edge of the property, her body angled toward something just beyond the fence line. Her ears were forward now, her posture alert in a way it hadn't been moments before. A warning.

Shea stepped off the deck immediately. "Heidi."

The dog didn't move.

Shea's pulse surged as she crossed the yard, her attention narrowing with each step. The air felt different now. Thicker, heavier, as if something unseen had shifted into place.

"Heidi," she said again, more firmly.

The dog turned her head slightly but didn't leave her position. That was enough.

Shea reached her side, her eyes following Heidi's line of sight—and stopped.

At first, it didn't register. It looked like nothing more than a scattering of flowers near the fence line. Pale, wilted, arranged in a loose circle against the grass.

But then, she saw the shape in the center. A body.

Her stomach dropped. "Stay," she said sharply to Heidi. The dog obeyed immediately.

Shea stepped forward, her breath tightening as the scene came into focus.

The victim lay on her back, her arms positioned at her sides, her clothing carefully arranged. Around her, wilted roses formed a rough circle, their petals darkened and beginning to curl at the edges.

Ash had been scattered between them, faint gray against the green grass. The smell hit her a moment later. Smoke, something burned.

Her chest tightened. "Ring around the rosie." The

words felt wrong in her mouth. Too soft for what she was looking at. She moved closer, her eyes scanning the victim's face.

Recognition came slowly. Then all at once. "God…"

It was Megan Doyle. Misty Hollow's local journalist.

The same one who had written the article questioning Shea's evidence ten years ago. The one who had cast doubt on the Morrison case when it mattered most.

"Shea?" Trevor's voice carried across the yard as his cruiser pulled in behind hers.

She didn't turn. "I found her."

A beat of silence.

Then Trevor moved quickly toward her, slowing only as he took in the scene.

Snelling and Webster arrived moments later, their expressions tightening as they stepped into the yard. Snelling crouched slightly, careful not to disturb anything. "Third victim."

"Yes," Shea said. "How did you know to come?"

"He called the office." Webster's gaze moved over the roses, the ash, the positioning. "This is escalating."

"No," Shea said quietly.

He looked at her.

"This is continuing."

Snelling glanced up. "Connection?"

"She covered the Morrison trial," Shea said.

"Wrote an article questioning the evidence. Suggested the case wasn't solid."

Webster nodded slowly. "So, in his mind, she contributed to the outcome."

"Yes."

Snelling's gaze shifted to the arrangement. "The roses… the ash…"

"Ring Around the Rosie," Trevor said.

"A pocket full of posies," Snelling added.

"And ashes, ashes," Webster finished.

The words hung heavy in the air.

Shea's eyes moved to the fence line behind the body. There—carved into the wood—the number **3**.

~

The sheriff's home represented something beyond safety. It was where she allowed herself distance from the work, where she stepped out of the role she carried every day. Which meant bringing the work to her changed the balance.

He had observed the property before. Not close enough to risk detection, but enough to understand the layout, the sightlines, the patterns of movement.

The dog had been the only variable. But even that had been manageable. Timing solved most problems. It always did.

The arrangement had been placed with the same care as the others. The roses chosen for their symbolism. The ash for its meaning. Decay and aftermath. What remained when something had already been lost.

He had left just before dawn, allowing the scene to settle into place before discovery. And then, he called.

He knew she would come outside. Knew she would look and understand.

That was the point. This was no longer about distance. It was about proximity.

And the closer she came to him, the clearer everything would become.

~

Trevor frowned. "Shea…he's coming to your home. He's coming for you."

"If I step back now, he wins," she said.

"That's not what this is about," Trevor replied.

"It is to him," she said.

Shea looked back at the body. At the roses and ash. At the number carved into the fence. Three.

Three victims. Three steps. And tomorrow, there would be another. Unless they stopped him. Where was he hiding? Somewhere close, she knew that much.

She straightened slowly, her voice steady. "Call it in," she said. "Full scene. We lock this down."

Trevor nodded and reached for his radio.

Snelling and Webster moved to begin coordinating.

Shea turned back toward the house, her jaw tightening. "Let's move."

Because the clock had already started ticking again. Actually, it hadn't stopped.

Chapter Six

Word had started to spread. First through official channels, then through the quiet, informal network that always moved faster. Three deaths in three days, all connected to a case most people thought had been buried. That the killer sat behind bars waiting to die.

By the time Shea stepped inside, she could feel it in the way people looked at her.

Not fear. Not yet. But something close. Expectation. The kind that came with a body count and no arrest, the kind that asked questions without saying them out loud.

She moved past it without slowing, heading straight for the bullpen. Trevor sat at his desk, a stack of files in front of him, phone tucked between his shoulder and ear. "Yeah. Pull everything you've got on alternates too. I don't care if they were dismissed day one. We're not assuming anything." He glanced up as she approached, held up a finger. "Right. Send it over."

He set the phone down and studied her for a moment. "You didn't sleep much."

"He left a body in my yard."

Trevor's jaw tightened. "Yeah."

"That changes things."

"I know."

She set her file down harder than she meant to, the sound sharp against the desk. "He's not just ahead of us anymore. He's inside this. He knows where I live, Trevor. He's been watching long enough to know my routine, my property, how close he can get without tripping anything." She paused. "That's not someone improvising."

"We'll adjust."

"We're reacting," she said. "Every time. He plans, we respond. He moves, we follow."

"That's how investigations work," Trevor said evenly.

"No." Her voice tightened. "That's how it works when we're losing."

The words hung there. Trevor let them sit, the way he always did when he thought she needed to hear herself.

"We're not losing," he said.

She met his eyes. "Then why are we three bodies in?"

Before he could respond, Snelling stepped into the bullpen, a tablet in her hand, Webster just behind her.

"We've got something," Snelling said.

"What?"

Snelling set the tablet on the desk and tapped the screen. "Phone records for all three victims — Vance, Hart, Doyle. There's a pattern. Unknown number. Repeated contact. Not calls — texts."

"How far back?" Trevor asked.

"Weeks."

That settled hard. Weeks of contact. Weeks of whatever this was, already in motion before the first body dropped.

"What do they say?" Shea asked.

Snelling turned the tablet so she could see.

The message thread was short and simple. No name, no identifying information — just a series of texts spaced days apart.

Do you remember the trial?

Do you remember what you decided? What they decided?

Do you remember what you said?

Something cold moved through her. "They all got this?"

"Yes," Snelling said. "Not all at once. Staggered. Timed."

"He was watching them," Trevor said.

"He was preparing them." Shea kept her eyes on the screen. Three questions, the same ones each time, building in sequence like steps down a staircase. Not threats. Not demands. Just reminders. As if the point wasn't to frighten them but to make sure they understood exactly why.

Snelling studied her. "You've seen this before?"

Shea shook her head. "Not like this." She had interviewed enough killers to know that the ones who planned this carefully weren't driven by rage. They were driven by something colder.

Webster tapped the edge of the tablet. "We're working on tracing the number, but it's routed through multiple layers. Whoever set this up knew what they were doing."

"Of course he did." Her gaze stayed on the messages.

Do you remember the trial?

Not just a question aimed at the victims. At everyone who had ever sat in that courtroom, everyone who had played a role in what happened, everyone who had walked away believing it was over.

At her.

Trevor pushed off the desk. "We need to get ahead of the next one."

"We start with the list," Shea said.

They had already begun assembling it, but now it took on a different weight.

Names filled the board — jurors, alternates, court staff, attorneys, witnesses. Each one a potential target. Each one a step in a sequence someone had been planning long enough to send text messages in the weeks before the first murder.

Shea stood in front of it. Her eyes moved from

name to name, trying to see the pattern from his perspective rather than her own.

Lila Vance — Jury Foreman. Evelyn Hart — Stenographer. Megan Doyle — Journalist. Harold Briggs — Bailiff.

Four roles. Four positions. Each connected not just to the trial itself, but to how it had been decided, documented, witnessed, and enforced. He wasn't picking people randomly or settling old scores by proximity. He was working through a structure. One he had mapped out carefully, one that meant something to him even if the logic wasn't yet visible to them.

"He's working outward," she said.

Trevor stepped beside her. "From decision to documentation to influence."

"And enforcement." She glanced at Briggs's name. A bailiff. The person responsible for maintaining order in the room where everything had gone wrong. "He's accounting for everyone who had a hand in it. Every function."

Snelling crossed her arms. "Then next would be what?"

Shea's gaze moved to the alternates listed lower on the board. Jurors who hadn't deliberated, but who had been present. Selected, seated, sworn in, and then sidelined. On standby. Watching the process play out from the edges.

"Someone who followed," she said.

Trevor frowned. "What do you mean?"

"The foreman leads. The others follow. He sees them as interchangeable." She paused, working it out as she spoke. "They showed up, they sat where they were told, they didn't question anything. He doesn't distinguish between them. To him, they're all the same."

Webster's expression sharpened. "Sheep."

The word landed flat and ugly. Shea nodded slowly. "Yes."

Before anyone could respond, Trevor's phone rang. He glanced at the screen. "Bolton." He listened, his expression shifting almost immediately. Something closed behind his eyes. "Where?" A pause. "Yeah. We're on our way."

He ended the call and looked at her. Nothing else needed saying.

The road cut through open land wide and quiet, broken only by fencing and the occasional stand of trees along the horizon. Patrol was already there when they arrived, parked near a break in the fence where the grass had been flattened.

Shea stepped out into the wind and took in the scene.

The body lay in the grass.

White. That was the first thing she noticed. White fabric, white wool, forced into the victim's mouth and left there like a signature.

She moved closer. The woman lay on her side, slightly curled, as if she had simply folded and never moved again. Hands drawn inward, fingers stiff, face turned toward the ground, pale against the dirt. No sign of a struggle in the immediate area. No drag marks. No indication she had tried to run.

She had come here willingly, or been brought here without realizing what was coming.

Snelling crouched near the body, her eyes moving over every detail in the methodical way she had. "No immediate signs of struggle."

Webster scanned the open ground around them. "Nothing for a quarter mile. No witnesses, no cover."

"She knew him," Trevor said.

"Or trusted him enough not to question it until it was too late." Shea's gaze moved to the fence post nearest the body. There — carved into the wood with something narrow and deliberate. The number 4.

She felt her breath catch.

"He's staying on sequence," Webster said.

She didn't look away from the carving. Four. Four days, four bodies, four roles accounted for. Which meant he already knew who came next.

Snelling leaned close to study the wool. "This was forced. Not placed after the fact."

Mary had a little lamb. Its fleece was white as snow.

The words arrived without invitation, the way things did when a pattern finally clicked into place. Shea's jaw tightened.

"Mary Had a Little Lamb," she said quietly.

Trevor was already pulling up the records on his phone. A moment passed. "Name's Carol Finch. Alternate juror. Morrison trial."

There it was. The next function in his sequence. Not a decision-maker, not a witness to history, just someone who had shown up and gone along with the process. A follower. A sheep.

Another role. Another piece locked into place.

~

He had not needed much preparation for this one.

Not because it mattered less, but because the structure was already established; once it existed, the rest followed its own logic. He had learned that early: begin with precision, and precision compounds.

She had been easier to approach than the others. Less guarded. She had received the messages the same as the rest, had sat with the same questions, but had not done what some of the others had done. She had not told anyone, had not changed her routines, had not started looking over her shoulder.

Perhaps she had decided the past was over.

He had corrected that impression.

He thought about the sheriff now. She would see this one quickly. The symbolism was simpler, more direct than the others. That was intentional. He wasn't hiding anymore. The closer she came to understanding the shape of what he was doing, the more clearly the next piece needed to present itself.

He wanted her to see. He needed her to.

That was the whole point.

~

Shea stood over the body, and the frustration rose in a way she couldn't keep entirely contained. "He's leading us."

Trevor glanced at her. "We're following the evidence."

"We're following *him*." She looked at the fence, at the carved number, at the wool left deliberately visible from the road. "Every step we take is one he already planned. He knew we'd pull the phone records. He knew we'd stand here trying to read the nursery rhyme. He's been three moves ahead since the first body dropped, and we keep playing catch-up like that's a sustainable strategy."

Trevor stepped closer. "That doesn't mean we can't close the gap."

"We should have seen this sooner. I should have seen it. When Pritchard walked, I told myself the case was over. That whatever came next was someone else's problem." She paused. "It wasn't."

"You had a case that fell apart," Trevor said, his voice even. "That's not the same as letting this happen."

She knew he was right. She also knew that knowing it and feeling it were two different things, and right now, she didn't have the energy to close that distance.

She looked back at the board in her mind — the names, the roles, the sequence still unfinished.

"We need Morrison," she said.

Trevor's attention sharpened. "We've already started the process—"

"Now," she cut in. "Not when the paperwork clears. Not after the next one turns up. *Now.*"

Snelling stepped closer. "You want to bring him in without a charge."

"I want to have a conversation," Shea said. "A long one."

Webster frowned. "We don't have enough to hold him. We don't even know where he is."

"I'm aware." She took a slow breath. "But if we wait until we have enough, and someone else dies in the meantime, we'll spend a long time explaining that decision. Find him." She looked at Trevor. "He's connected. Maybe not directly, but he's in this somewhere. Someone is doing this *for* a reason, and that reason has Morrison's name on it."

Trevor held her gaze for a long moment, then nodded once. "We'll find him."

"We don't *find* him," Shea said. "We go get him."

The wind moved across the pasture, bending the grass in long, slow waves. Somewhere distant, a bird called out once and went quiet.

Shea looked down at Carol Finch one last time. Alternate juror, follower, the fourth name in a sequence that wasn't finished, and felt something settle inside her. Something like focus sharpening after a long period of blur.

She had spent three days reacting. Reading his signs, working his crime scenes, following the thread he had chosen to lay out for her.

But she knew the list now. She knew the structure. And if she knew the structure, she could stop waiting for the next body and start deciding where she was going to be when he moved.

For the first time since this began, she wasn't just following the pattern.

She was starting to think about it.

74

Chapter Seven

The rain started sometime before dawn. Just a steady, cold drizzle that settled over Misty Hollow and didn't seem interested in leaving anytime soon. By the time Shea pulled into the station parking lot, the sky had gone flat gray, pressing low and close, making the town feel smaller than usual. Contained.

She cut the engine but didn't move. Four bodies. Four days. And somewhere inside the pattern she hadn't fully decoded yet, the next one already waiting.

Her phone sat silent on the console. That almost made it worse.

A knock on the passenger window broke through it. Trevor stood there, rain darkening his jacket at the shoulders, one hand braced lightly against the glass. He gave her a look she recognized. Not pity or not alarm. Just the steady acknowledgment of someone who had seen her carry things before and knew better than to make a production of it.

She unlocked the door. He slid in, bringing a faint

chill of damp air, and pulled the door shut without a word. For a moment, neither of them spoke. Then he reached over and lifted her coffee cup from the holder, just slightly, as if checking the weight of it.

"You didn't drink this," he said.

"I forgot."

"You don't forget coffee." A smile teased at his lips.

She returned his smile with the hint of one of her own before it faded. "Guess there's a first time."

He set the cup back and leaned against the seat, studying her with the patience that had always irritated her slightly when she was fine and meant everything when she wasn't.

"You okay?" he asked.

Simple question. It always was with him.

She stared forward, watching the rain blur the edges of the world beyond the glass. "No." The honesty surprised her a little. She didn't take it back.

Trevor didn't rush to fill the silence. He let the answer exist between them, unchallenged, which was its own kind of relief. Then, quietly: "Good."

She turned to him. "Good?"

"If you were fine, I'd be worried."

That pulled a small, real smile from her, brief, but real. She looked away again. "He's still ahead of us."

"I know."

"And we're not catching up."

"We are," he said. "You just can't feel it yet."

She didn't argue. It didn't feel that way. But Trevor had a different relationship with patience than she did, and she had learned over the years that he wasn't always wrong. Rarely, actually.

He reached over and rested his hand lightly over hers on the steering wheel. Just that. Just enough to anchor her.

Shea stilled. The contact was warm and steady, and it cut through the tension in a way no amount of coffee or forward motion had managed to.

"You don't have to carry all of it alone," he said.

Her throat tightened unexpectedly. "I know." Knowing and believing, she thought, were not the same thing.

He gave her hand a brief squeeze, then let go and sat back, easy and matter-of-fact, as if it had just been the practical thing to do. "Come on," he said. "Let's get inside before you start blaming your mood on the weather."

"Don't tempt me."

Inside, Snelling and Webster stood near the bullpen with one of the deputies, speaking in low voices over a map that had been pulled up on the board. Four pins marked four locations, each annotated with names, dates, and the particulars of what had been left behind.

Shea stepped closer, her eyes moving over the geography of it.

He hadn't been choosing people at random. She had understood that from early on. But looking at the map now, she saw something else.

"He's not just choosing people," she said. "He's choosing where."

Snelling nodded. "We noticed. The locations are spread far enough to avoid immediate overlap but close enough that the pattern's legible."

"He wants us to connect them," Trevor said.

"Yes." Shea's gaze moved from pin to pin. "He's been deliberate about that from the start. The symbols, the nursery rhymes, the sequence…none of it is for his benefit. It's for ours."

Webster crossed his arms. "Which means he's communicating something."

"He's been communicating since the first body," Shea said. "We've just been too focused on the victims to hear it clearly."

She had been through the Morrison case file three times in the past forty-eight hours, reading backward from what she knew now. Something had been bothering her in a way she hadn't yet been able to articulate. She turned to the board and tried.

"He's not just targeting roles," she said. "He's targeting influence. The foreman led the jury. The stenographer recorded everything — created the official record. The journalist shaped what the public believed about the trial. The bailiff maintained the order of the room itself." She paused. "And the alternate juror followed along without question."

Snelling's expression sharpened. "He's mapping

everyone who determined how that trial was experienced. Not just decided."

Shea nodded. "Which tells us the next target isn't someone peripheral. It's someone whose influence on the outcome was specific."

Trevor frowned. "Who's left?"

She didn't answer immediately. Because she wasn't sure. And that, more than anything else in the past four days, was what kept her up at night.

Her phone rang. The sound cut through the room, and every head turned. Shea felt her pulse spike as she pulled it out.

Unknown number.

Trevor's eyes found hers. She answered before he could say anything.

"This is Sheriff Callahan."

Silence. Then the same slow, controlled breathing as before, unhurried, as if someone had nowhere else to be. "You're thinking too narrowly," he said.

Her jaw tightened. "Then help me think more broadly."

A pause. Long enough that she thought he might hang up. "You're looking at what they did," he said. "Not what they meant."

Her eyes went to the board. "What's the difference?"

"Everything."

Another pause.

"What does that mean?" she asked.

"You'll see." The line went dead.

She lowered the phone slowly and turned to face the room. Everyone watched her.

"He said we're looking at what they did," she said. "Not what they meant."

Snelling frowned. "He's assigning them symbolic roles beyond their actual function."

"Or rewriting the roles altogether," Webster said.

Shea stared at the board. "He's not correcting the trial. He's correcting the story. In his version, every person who contributed to him walking free is responsible. Not just legally — morally. And he's working through them one by one."

The room went quiet.

Trevor's radio crackled before anyone could respond.

Unit three. Possible fall at the courthouse steps. Male victim. Severe head trauma. Scene appears... unusual.

Shea dashed for the door.

The courthouse loomed against the gray sky, its stone steps sheened with rain. Emergency lights pulsed at the bottom of the staircase, washing pale color across the wet surface. Officers had already established a perimeter.

Shea stepped out of the cruiser and looked up.

The man lay at the base of the stairs, his body angled wrong in the way that meant the fall had been fast and final. His head was turned sharply to one side.

Around him, scattered across the wet stone, were fragments of something white — small, curved pieces, broken and spread across the steps in a rough radius.

Trevor stepped beside her. "That's not a fall."

"No," she said.

They moved closer. The fragments came into focus as they approached — ceramic, off-white, deliberately shattered. Some pieces were larger, some reduced nearly to dust. At the center of the debris, a few curved shards still held their shape, like the crown of something that had once been whole.

An egg.

Shea felt the nursery rhyme arrive before she consciously reached for it. "Humpty Dumpty."

Trevor exhaled beside her. "Sat on a wall."

"Had a great fall," Snelling said, her voice flat.

Webster remained quiet for a moment, looking at the steps, at the body, at the broken pieces scattered like punctuation. "All the king's horses and all the king's men."

"Couldn't put him back together again," Shea finished.

The words landed with a weight that none of them moved to break. She stood and glanced at the courthouse doors. At what the building represented, at the system that had been housed inside it, at the outcome that had come out of it.

"Who is he?" she asked.

One of the officers stepped forward. "Daniel

Reeves. Appellate attorney."

Trevor's expression shifted. "Morrison case?"

"Yes, sir. He argued the procedural technicality that resulted in Morrison's release."

The silence that followed was different from the ones before it.

Snelling said quietly, "He didn't just participate in the trial."

"He changed the ending," Webster said.

Shea's gaze moved to the stone wall beside the steps. There, carved into the surface with the same deliberate precision as every mark before it, the number 5. Five. She looked at it for a long moment. Five days. Five victims. Five corrections in a sequence that wasn't finished.

And Reeves hadn't been at the original trial. He had come after, finding the crack in the foundation, leveraged it, and walked Morrison out the door. In the logic of whoever was doing this, that made him worse than the rest. Not complicit in the verdict. Responsible for undoing the one consequence that had survived it.

She understood, suddenly, what the call had meant.

Not what they did. What they meant.

Reeves hadn't played a role in the trial. He had played a role in the story — the final chapter, the one where the system failed in the most visible and irreversible way possible. To someone keeping score, that mattered more than anything that had happened in the courtroom itself.

But why would Morrison kill, not keeping it a secret that he was the one doing the murders, when he'd walked free? What could be his motive behind it all?

~

This one had required a different kind of patience.

The others had been present at the moment of failure. Reeves had arrived after — and made failure permanent. There was a distinction. He had weighed it carefully.

The fall was appropriate. Not just in symbol but in logic. Something that had stood and then collapsed. Something that could not be reassembled by any amount of effort or authority.

The sheriff was close now. Closer than she realized.

He wasn't concerned. He wanted her close.

~

Rain continued to fall, washing over the stone steps, over the broken ceramic, over the edges of everything.

Trevor appeared beside her. "You're putting it together."

"I think so." She kept her eyes on the scene. "He's not working through the trial. He's working through the outcome. Everyone who contributed — directly or indirectly — to him going free."

"Then the list is longer than we thought," Trevor said.

"Yes." She turned to face the board in her mind.

All the names, all the functions, all the people who had touched that case and walked away believing it was finished. "And he's already further through it than we are."

Snelling stepped closer. "Then we move faster."

"We move smarter," Shea said. "Faster is what he's expecting."

She looked once more at Daniel Reeves. At the broken pieces around him, at the courthouse steps slick with rain, at the number carved into stone that would still be there long after the scene was processed and cleared.

She thought about what Trevor had said in the car. *You can't feel it yet.*

Maybe. But something had shifted in the past hour. Something quiet and internal, less like momentum and more like clarity. She didn't just read the scene anymore. She was reading him. The logic underneath it, the story he told himself, the destination he had already chosen.

If she knew where he was going, she could stop waiting for the next body and start deciding where she was going to be when he arrived. She turned away from the steps.

"Go over the full Morrison case roster again," she said. "Everyone. Defense team, prosecution, court staff, appeals record. Everyone whose name appears anywhere in that file."

Trevor nodded. "And Morrison himself?"

She thought about it.

"Especially Morrison," she said.

The rain kept falling. Somewhere beyond the gray sky and the courthouse steps and the broken pieces of ceramic on wet stone, the next move was already in progress.

But for the first time in five days, Shea felt she was beginning to think within the pattern rather than around its edges.

That wasn't catching up.

That was something better.

Chapter Eight

The call came mid-morning.

Shea had just started to feel the investigation shift beneath her with less reaction and more pattern. The difference between being pulled along by a current and finally getting a read on where it was headed when Trevor's phone rang across the bullpen. She didn't need to ask. She saw it in the set of his jaw as he listened, the way his hand tightened on the phone turning his knuckles white before he ended the call.

"Fall festival warehouse." He reached for his jacket. "An employee found something in storage."

"How bad?"

He hesitated just long enough. "Bad. Staged."

Snelling and Webster were already moving. No one spoke on the way out. After five scenes, the silence before arrival had become its own kind of preparation. A way of setting aside everything you thought you understood so the scene could tell you what it actually was.

The warehouse sat just outside town, a long, low building used for seasonal storage — decorations, displays, everything that turned Misty Hollow into something postcard-perfect each fall and holiday. It stood quiet now, a single patrol car idling near the loading doors. An employee waited off to the side, pale and hugging herself, her gaze somewhere past all of them.

Shea stepped out and caught the smell immediately. Not decay — too soon for that. Something earthier. Wet vegetation. The sweetness of cut pumpkin left too long in the air.

Trevor fell into step beside her. "You doing all right?"

"Ask me after." She marched to the door.

The warehouse door groaned as they pushed it open, the sound swallowed quickly by the high ceiling and the rows of stacked seasonal inventory beyond. Wooden crates, bundled hay, strings of artificial lights, and decorative arrangements waiting to be set out. It smelled like fall and something very wrong underneath it.

Shea slowed as they moved toward the far end.

The display was elaborate with dozens of pumpkins arranged across a wide stretch of floor, some carved, some whole, others stacked in loose decorative piles. Real thought had been put into the presentation. At the center of it, one oversized pumpkin stood apart from the rest, its proportions slightly off, its carved face turned outward as if it were looking at whoever came through the door.

She felt the shape of it before her mind fully named it. "There."

They approached carefully. The pumpkin was large enough that at first it simply looked like a display piece waiting to be positioned somewhere prominent. But the edges of the carved opening were too deliberate, the lid sitting slightly too neat, and the faint smell rose stronger here.

Trevor brushed his hand across Shea's lower back, then reached the far side and crouched to look at the base. "He spent time on this."

Shea nodded.

Snelling moved in close, examining the cuts with careful eyes. "Clean work. No jagged edges, no mistakes. This wasn't done in a hurry."

Webster had already moved out to scan the broader scene. "No disturbance anywhere else in the building. No overturned crates, nothing displaced."

"Same pattern," Trevor said. "He came in knowing exactly what he was going to do."

Shea studied the lid. "Open it."

Trevor positioned himself, lifted it carefully, and set it aside. The smell thickened.

The victim had been seated, shoulders hunched forward under the forced geometry of the space, head tilted slightly down, expression frozen somewhere between surprise and resignation. His clothing was rumpled but not torn. No blood visible. No defensive marks on his hands. He had been put here after.

"Peter, Peter, Pumpkin Eater," Shea said quietly.

Trevor exhaled through his nose. "Had a wife and couldn't keep her."

Snelling finished it, her voice low. "He put her in a pumpkin shell, and there he kept her well."

Shea stepped closer to Trevor, welcoming his warm strength. Despite them vowing to keep their personal relationship separate from their job, his arm snaked around her waist, bringing her a bit of comfort.

The silence that followed was different from the others. Not heavier, exactly, but textured differently. There was something almost domestic about the nursery rhyme, something that made this feel more intimate than the courthouse steps or the pasture road. More patient.

"Who is he?" Shea asked.

The officer near the door stepped forward. "Richard Hale. Judge's clerk." The words settled in.

"He worked directly under the judge assigned to the Morrison case," the officer continued. "Handled all case documentation. Had full access to chambers communications, scheduling, everything that moved through the judge's office."

Trevor looked at her. "That's closer to the center than any of them."

"Yes, it is." She glanced back at Hale. In the nursery rhyme, the pumpkin shell was a prison. A place where something inconvenient was kept out of sight. She wondered if that was how the killer thought of Hale. Not as someone who had acted, but as someone who had contained. Who had helped the system keep its secrets in the dark.

She turned toward the small desk set up along the wall — a working space, cluttered with storage logs and a laptop sitting open and dark.

"His?" she asked.

The employee nodded. "He handled all the inventory for the festival. Been doing it for years. Very organized."

Shea gestured to Webster, who moved in and brought the laptop to life. The login screen flickered, then gave way to a desktop with folders arranged with the neatness of someone who had built their entire professional identity around keeping things ordered.

"Look through it," she said.

Nodding, Webster scanned the folders, then paused. He clicked once, then again. The folder opened.

Inside, there were documents that had no business being stored in a warehouse laptop for a fall festival inventory system.

Court records. Scanned filings. Typed notes in a format she recognized from case documentation. Transcripts.

"These are sealed records," Snelling said, her voice tight.

Shea leaned in closer, reading the file names. Jury

deliberation notes. Internal chamber communications. A folder labeled *Suppressed — Pre-Trial* that shouldn't have existed outside the courthouse archives, let alone here.

Trevor stood behind her shoulder. "He copied them."

"Over the years, by the look of it." Shea straightened slowly. "He had access through the judge's office. He knew what the records contained. And he kept them. here, off-site, outside the official system."

"Why would he do that?" Snelling asked.

It was the right question. Shea didn't answer it yet. She still turned it over, feeling the shape of it, the way it didn't quite fit the picture of someone who was simply complicit. Complicit people kept their heads down and destroyed evidence. They didn't catalog it.

"He wasn't protecting himself," she said. "He was documenting."

Webster looked at her. "Documenting what?"

"Everything that went wrong." She looked at the folders again. "Every place the case lost integrity. Every point of failure." She paused. "He knew where the weaknesses were."

Trevor's voice was careful. "You're saying Morrison knew too."

"I'm saying someone needed Hale to have this information," she said. "And I don't think Hale was the one who decided to keep it."

~

He had been patient with this one longer than any of the others.. Hale had been useful — conscientious, and organized, the kind of man who believed in systems and trusted the people above him in them. That trust had made him easy to work with. It had also made him easy to overlook.

The documents had confirmed what he already knew. But confirmation still mattered. It closed the circle on each piece.

The pumpkin had been Hale's own idea, in a way. He had arranged this space himself, tended it year after year, kept everything in its place. There was a certain appropriateness to using the structure he had built.

The sheriff was reading it correctly now. He could feel it in the way each scene had tightened the lens.

She was no longer looking at what he had done. She was beginning to see why, and soon it would be her turn to pay.

~

"He's been inside this for years," Trevor said. "Not following it. Not watching from the outside." He looked at the screen. "He built something."

"He built a case," Shea said. "Not to prosecute, but to control. He needed to know exactly where the system was fragile so he could decide when and how it failed."

Snelling stepped closer. "You're saying the trial didn't fall apart by accident."

"I'm saying I don't believe in that much coincidence anymore." Shea looked at the suppressed evidence folder. "These documents show the case losing structural integrity at specific points. Procedural errors that were just large enough to matter. Evidentiary problems that emerged at exactly the right moments."

Webster frowned. "You think the failures were engineered."

"I think Morrison didn't need to escape the system," she said. "I also don't think he wanted the system to fail visibly, on the record, in a way that couldn't be challenged." She paused. "Because then the outcome belongs to the system. Not to him. He wants us to stop him."

Trevor said quietly, "You're saying he didn't want to go free."

"That's exactly what I'm saying."

"And now he's killing them," Snelling said. "Because he believes, that together, they all failed."

"Maybe. We do know someone is killing them," Shea said.

Trevor looked at her sharply. "You're separating Morrison from the murders."

"I'm keeping the possibility open," she said. "Because if Morrison needed the trial to fail, he needed those people alive and quiet — not dead and drawing attention back to the case."

Webster's expression shifted. "Then who—"

"Someone who found out what happened," Shea said. "Someone who knows what those documents contain and decided that the system failing quietly wasn't justice." She let that sit for a moment. "Someone who thinks they're finishing what the trial should have started." She said the words, but didn't believe them. Her gut told her Morrison did the killing. That he no longer wanted a partner, but as sheriff, she couldn't overlook any possibilities.

Trevor was quiet for a long moment. Then: "That's a different kind of killer than we've been building a profile for."

"Yes," she said. "It is. If it's true. We can't just focus on Morrison. Not until he outright says it's him."

She looked once more at Richard Hale, clerk, keeper of records, a man who had spent years maintaining the meticulous archive of his own complicity, and then turned away.

"Pull everything off that laptop," she said to Webster. "I want every file cross-referenced against the original case record." She looked at Snelling. "And get me the full list of anyone who had access to the judge's chambers during the Morrison trial. Staff, interns, temporary personnel. Everyone."

Snelling nodded and moved.

Trevor fell into step beside Shea as she headed toward the door. "You said we were looking for Morrison like he was hiding. Now you're saying someone else might be running this."

"I'm saying Morrison isn't hiding," she said. "I don't think he ever was. I think he's been exactly where he wants to be the entire time." She pushed through the warehouse door into the gray afternoon, the damp air caught at her jacket. "The question isn't where Morrison is."

Trevor waited.

"It's who else knew what he did," she said. "And what they're willing to do about it."

The sky above Misty Hollow was still flat and gray, the same low ceiling it had been all morning. But the shape of what lay beneath it had changed completely.

Chapter Nine

The next morning came too fast.

Shea woke before her alarm. For a moment, she lay still, staring at the ceiling, her body heavy and her mind already moving through the case as it had never stopped.

Then the awareness settled in. Another day. Which meant the clock had already started.

Her phone sat on the nightstand, the screen dark and silent. She stared at it like something she couldn't trust despite its apparent innocence. He had said one every day. Six days in, he hadn't deviated. The silence didn't mean nothing had happened. It meant she hadn't been told yet.

From the other side of the bed, Heidi lifted her head. Shea reached down and let her fingers move through the dog's fur, grounding herself in the warmth and solidity of it. "I know, girl.".

Heidi huffed once and settled her chin on the mattress, keeping watch.

Shea pushed upright, muscles protesting the inadequate rest, and reached for her phone. No missed calls. No messages. Nothing. She stood at the window for a moment; the morning outside was clear again. The light came in low and clean across the yard where this had all started.

Either the next murder hadn't happened yet. Or it had, and they just hadn't found it.

She was dressed and out the door in twelve minutes.

Trevor sat at his desk when she walked in, a cup of coffee waiting on the edge of it that he slid toward her without looking up from the file in front of him. She took it without comment, wrapping both hands around it, though the warmth was more comfort than remedy.

"You didn't sleep," he said.

"Some."

He looked up. "Some meaning what exactly?"

"Meaning I'm here and functional. Don't push it."

The corner of his mouth moved slightly. He let it go.

"Anything come in?" she asked.

"Not yet."

The words settled uncomfortably. Six mornings of the same rhythm — arrive, wait, get the call, go to the scene. The pattern had become its own kind of dread, the anticipation almost as heavy as the arrival. She set her coffee down and moved to the board.

Six names. Six roles. Six scenes processed under

skies that had finally cleared, as if the weather had decided it had set an appropriate enough backdrop and could afford to stop pressing. The board looked the same as it had when she'd left last night, but she had learned that looking at it with fresh eyes sometimes rearranged what she thought she understood.

Not this morning. This morning, it looked exactly like what it was: a sequence with entries still remaining.

Snelling and Webster came in together, already talking, already working. "Morrison's financials." Snelling set a folder on the nearest desk. "We went deeper. He's been careful — very careful — but there are transfers in the eighteen months prior to the trial that don't have clean origins."

"How much?" Trevor asked.

"Enough to matter. Small enough to stay under standard thresholds, frequent enough to suggest ongoing arrangement rather than a one-time transaction." She paused. "He was paying for something in the lead-up to the trial."

"Or someone," Webster said.

Shea looked at the transfers. "Which means the engineering started earlier than we thought. He wasn't improvising as the trial developed. He had the framework in place before it began."

"Which fits Crane's role," Trevor said. "A junior paralegal with access to document transfers between the defense and the judge's office. That's not something you recruit at the last minute. "

Shea nodded. "He built the apparatus first. Then he built the case inside it."

Before anyone could follow that thread further, Trevor's radio crackled.

Unit three — possible DOA at the county daycare on Willow Lane. Staff member found unresponsive. Scene appears staged. Like the others.

Trevor exhaled quietly. "There it is."

Shea reached for her jacket. Her heart lay like a stone in the pit of her stomach.

The daycare sat at the edge of a quiet residential street, t, low-roofed and painted in warm yellows and greens, with a hand-painted mural of animals along the front exterior that the morning sun hit at an angle, making it look almost cheerful. The yellow tape going up across the entrance contradicted it.

A single patrol car sat in the nearly empty lot. The officer at the tape was young, holding his composure with the careful effort of someone who hadn't been at many scenes like this.

"Who found her?" Shea ducked under the tape.

"Another staff member. Came in early to set up for the day. Said at first she thought someone had left a decoration out overnight." He paused. "Then she got closer."

Shea pushed the front door open. The smell reached her immediately — something sweet and artificial layered over the underlying scent of the building itself, crayons and disinfectant, and the warmth of a space designed for small children. Beneath the sweetness, something faintly chemical. Not strong. Not obvious. Just present enough to register.

The hallway was lined with children's artwork — construction-paper suns with tissue-paper rays, painted handprints arranged in arcs across the wall, stick figures holding hands beneath careful block-letter names. Smiling faces everywhere. The work of children who believed the world was the size of this hallway and entirely good.

Shea's throat tightened as she moved past them. She kept her eyes forward.

The room at the end of the hall stood open.

She slowed before she reached the doorway, a habit that made her take in the frame before the full scene. Then she stepped through.

The victim sat in a rocking chair positioned near the window, placed to catch the morning light. Her body leaned slightly to one side, her head tilted, her arms resting loosely in her lap. At first glance, she might have been sleeping, but the absolute quality of it gave it away immediately.

Above her, hanging from a ceiling beam on a length of fabric was a bundle, shaped loosely like a cradle. Empty. Swaying almost imperceptibly in the air current from the open door.

Shea felt something cold move through her chest. "Rock-a-bye baby." .

Trevor's voice came from just behind her. "On the

treetop."

Snelling stepped into the room, took in the scene, and finished it softly. "When the wind blows, the cradle will rock."

Webster's gaze moved from the hanging fabric to the victim. "When the bough breaks, the cradle will fall."

"And down will come baby…" Shea didn't finish the line. The room had finished it for her.

She stood still for a moment, letting the scene resolve into its details. The rocking chair had been positioned with the same deliberate precision as every scene before it. Nothing accidental, nothing incidental, every element chosen for what it contributed to the composition. No signs of struggle anywhere in the room. No overturned furniture, no disruption to the organized bins of toys and supplies along the far wall. The victim's clothing was neat, her expression neutral in the way that sedation before death sometimes produced.

"Cause of death?" she asked.

The officer near the door checked his notes. "Preliminary suggests sedation followed by suffocation. Medical examiner is en route."

Controlled, Shea thought. Again.

"Who is she?" Trevor asked.

The officer read from his notes. "Laura Bennett. Part-time staff here for the past three years."

Trevor was already on his phone, running the

name. Shea watched his expression shift as the results populated.

"She's in the Morrison file," he said.

"Witness?"

"Character witness for the prosecution. Testified about Jennifer Morrison, specifically about the pattern of abuse. She knew Jennifer through a community group, had observed the relationship over two years, and corroborated the documented incidents." He paused. "Her testimony was considered one of the stronger pieces of the prosecution's case."

Shea looked at Laura Bennett — at the careful stillness, at the hanging cradle above her, at the morning light coming through the window across both of them. She thought about what it meant to be chosen for this scene specifically. Not a juror, not a court official, not someone inside the machinery of the trial's collapse. Someone who had stood up and told Jennifer's story in front of a room full of people who had ultimately decided it wasn't enough.

"She gave Jennifer a voice," Shea said.

Webster nodded. "When almost no one else did."

"And she still ended up here," Snelling said quietly.

Shea turned toward the wall behind the rocking chair. She had been expecting it, and there it was — carved lightly into the paint with the same precise instrument as every other mark, clean-edged and intentional.

The number 7.

Seven days. Seven deaths. Seven chapters in a story that kept insisting it wasn't finished.

She stared at it for a long moment. Then she turned back to the room. To the cradle and the children's artwork visible through the door in the hallway beyond, to the sunlight lying across a scene designed to mean something specific, and to think about what that meaning actually was.

~

The space had been chosen for what it represented, not for what it was.

Innocence. Care. The belief that certain places are exempt from the worst things people do to each other. He had no interest in that belief.

Laura Bennett had spoken clearly. Her voice had been calm, credible, and sympathetic in a way that had moved the room. He had watched from the gallery and understood exactly what she contributed. Not to justice, as she believed, but to the story. His story. The one he had been constructing long before she took the stand.

She had been useful. Now she was necessary in a different way.

The sheriff was in the room now. He knew that without seeing it. He could feel the investigation's weight shifting toward him, the distance between them compressing with each scene.

Good. He needed her close. He needed her to understand her failure before it ended.

~

Snelling pulled up the court roster on her tablet. "We've accounted for the foreman, the stenographer, the journalist, the bailiff, the alternate juror, the appellate attorney, the clerk." She looked up. "Laura Bennett doesn't fit that sequence. She's outside the trial's internal structure."

"He's expanding the frame," Trevor said.

Shea shook her head. "No. He's been consistent from the beginning. He's targeting everyone who contributed to the outcome. Not just the people who made decisions inside the courtroom. Everyone whose participation shaped what happened regarding Jennifer's death and what happened to Morrison afterward." She looked at Bennett. "Laura told Jennifer's story in a room that didn't listen. In his logic, she's part of why the failure mattered. Because the evidence was there, the testimony was there, and the system still failed."

"So, he's punishing the system through the people who tried to hold it up," Webster said.

"He's finishing the story," Shea said. "His version of it. The one where every person who touched this case gets accounted for, regardless of which side they were on."

Shea stepped away from the wall, away from the number, and moved back toward the door. In the hallway, the painted handprints ran along the wall in their careful arcs, the block-lettered names of children who would arrive in a few hours to find their daycare wrapped in tape and their teacher gone.

"Pull everyone remaining on the unaccounted roster," she said. "Anyone whose name appears in the Morrison file in any capacity — prosecution, defense, witnesses, court staff, media coverage. Anyone." She looked at Trevor. "And I want a map. All seven activation points from his calls and all seven scene locations overlaid. We have got to provide protection."

Trevor nodded. "I'll have it inside an hour."

She looked once more at Laura Bennett, at the cradle swaying gently in the disturbed air of the room, at the morning light that had no business being as clean and bright as it was across a scene like this.

"She told the truth," Shea said quietly. Not to anyone in particular. Just to the room. "She came into that courtroom and told exactly what she had seen, and it wasn't enough, and now she's here."

No one responded. There wasn't anything to respond with.

Shea marched back down the hallway past the painted suns and the smiling stick figures and the careful work of children who believed the world was safe, pushed through the front door, and stood in the full morning sunlight with her hands at her sides.

The sky above Misty Hollow was clear and limitless. The world looked its most open and uncomplicated on the seventh day of the worst case she had worked in years. Ever.

Trevor came out behind her and stood close enough that his shoulder almost touched hers, both of them facing the parking lot and the quiet residential street beyond it. "He's not slowing down."

"No." He's keeping to his word."

"But you're getting closer."

"Am I?" She looked at him. "We know who it is, what he's doing. I understand the logic of it, but what I don't have yet is where he goes after the list is finished." She paused. "Because I don't think the list ending is the ending. And…I have no idea where he is."

The sun moved another degree across the sky, the shadows in the parking lot shifting slightly, the ordinary world continuing its business around the edges of everything they were standing inside.

"Then we step it up on finding Morrison," Trevor said.

She nodded and turned back toward the building — toward the work, toward the board, toward the name at the center of it all, which they hadn't yet found in the physical world, despite knowing exactly where he existed in the logic of the case.

The morning was clear, and the day already moved, and somewhere in Misty Hollow, the next chapter was being written by someone who had decided long ago how the story would end.

Shea intended to change that ending before he got there.

Chapter Ten

Shea stood on her deck the next morning after yet another restless sleep, coffee in hand, and watched as Heidi roamed the yard. Somewhere in Misty Hollow, a man who had not deviated once from his sequence was already inside his next day.

She turned and entered the house, rinsed out her coffee cup, called to Heidi, then donned her gun holster and jacket. Time to start another day in a fruitless search for Morrison.

The drive in was quiet. The morning sun still hung low enough to come through the windshield at an angle that required the visor. Two consecutive clear days after the gray week that had preceded them. The town looked like itself in this light — the brick storefronts on the main street, the courthouse visible above the tree line, the ordinary weekday rhythm of a place that continued its business regardless of what happened at its edges. She had always found that both comforting and faintly surreal. Life persisting.

Unaware, or choosing not to be.

She pulled into the station lot and sat for a moment before getting out, gazing at the building in the early light, thinking about what was waiting inside. The board, the roster, the names still unaccounted for, and the sequence that had its own logic she understood better each day without yet being able to see its end.

With a heavy exhale, she got out and went in.

Trevor stood at the coffee machine, sleeves already rolled, one hand braced on the counter while it finished brewing. He glanced up as she came through the door. "You didn't sleep again,"

"I slept some." She accepted the cup of coffee he held out to her.

"Some being?"

"Enough to be here. Stop mothering me." She wrapped both hands around the cup and felt the warmth work its way in. "Nothing came in?"

"Not yet. Just like yesterday. He's waiting until after dark to contact us now."

She looked at the board through the bullpen doorway. At the numbers carved into different surfaces across Misty Hollow. The sequence was visible now in a way it hadn't been at the beginning, each piece clarifying the ones around it, the whole thing resolving slowly into a shape she could almost hold in full.

Almost.

"He's already moving," she said.

"Probably." Trevor didn't offer the reassurance

she hadn't asked for. That was one of the things she trusted most about him.

Snelling came in from the side corridor with Webster just behind her, both of them carrying the focused energy of people who had been working before they arrived.

"Media archives." Snelling set a folder on the nearest desk. "We went back through every piece of coverage from the Morrison trial — articles, follow-up interviews, opinion pieces, anything with a byline or a named source."

Webster placed a second folder beside it. "One name kept appearing in a way that didn't fit the standard coverage pattern."

"Daniel Pierce," Snelling said. "Alternate juror. He sat through the entire trial but wasn't called to deliberate. Fourteen months after the verdict, he gave one interview — a local piece, buried, never picked up anywhere else."

Shea took the folder and opened it. The interview transcript was three pages, annotated in Snelling's precise hand with yellow highlights at specific passages.

She found the one that mattered on the second page. *He wanted us to believe something.*

She read it twice. Then she read the lines around it, the context Pierce had given — halting, and uncertain. "He noticed."

Trevor leaned in beside her to read it. She was

aware of the proximity — his shoulder close to hers, the slight warmth of it.

"He noticed something was off," Trevor said, "but he couldn't name it."

"He was an alternate," Snelling said. "He couldn't deliberate, couldn't influence the verdict, couldn't do anything except sit there and watch."

"Which made him exactly the kind of witness Morrison couldn't fully control," Shea said. "Someone observing from the outside of the process rather than inside it. Someone who might eventually talk." She looked at the highlighted line again. *He wanted us to believe something.* "He almost understood. That's worse than not understanding at all…if you're someone who needs this buried."

Webster crossed his arms. "So, Pierce gets the call fourteen months after the trial, gives one interview that barely gets read, and fourteen months after that—"

Trevor's radio crackled.

Unit three — possible DOA at private residence off Ridge Lane. Male found unresponsive. Caller is a neighbor. Scene appears staged. Same type of call as all the days before.

"That's Pierce," Trevor said.

The house sat at the end of a narrow gravel road, trees pressed close on both sides, giving it a sense of privacy despite its proximity to town. The morning light didn't reach well here — too much canopy, the angle still too low — and the shade gave the scene a different quality than the ones before it. Closer. More contained.

A neighbor stood near the patrol car, arms wrapped around herself despite the relative warmth of the morning. Her face carried the expression of someone who had found something they couldn't un-find.

"She came to check on him," the officer said as Shea approached. "Said he hadn't answered calls in two days."

Two days? Shea nodded and pushed through the front door.

The house was ordered. That was the first thing she noticed. Books aligned on shelves, papers stacked with neatness on a desk visible through the study doorway, everything in its place, suggested someone who had built their domestic life around the comfort of organization. A man who had sat through an entire trial, taking careful mental notes, and spent ten years trying to make sense of what he had observed.

The living room stopped her at the doorway.

Daniel Pierce sat in a chair positioned near the center of the room. His head tilted slightly forward, expression frozen, eyes half-lidded in the blankness of sedation before death.

Around the chair, across the floor in an irregular pattern that spread toward every wall were small white figurines. Sheep.

Dozens of them. Ceramic, plastic, and carved

wood, different scales and styles, as if collected from everywhere and assembled here for this specific purpose. They faced inward, outward, sideways — a scattered flock without a shepherd, displaced and directionless around the still figure in the chair.

Shea stood in the doorway and felt the meaning of it arrive before she reached for the words. "Little Bo Peep."

Trevor exhaled behind her. "Has lost her sheep."

"And doesn't know where to find them," Snelling finished, her voice careful.

Webster looked at the figurines spread across the floor. "Leave them alone, and they'll come home."

The rigidity of the corpse suggested he'd been sitting there for a couple of days, something the ME could determine for sure. "Why kill him earlier and only let us know today?" Shea stepped into the room. The sheep weren't random. Up close, the arrangement had a logic — they were densest nearest the chair and thinned toward the walls, as if the flock had been dispersing outward from the center, walking away from something or something walking away from them.

They weren't lost, she thought. They had been led somewhere they didn't know they were going.

She looked at Pierce. No defensive marks. No signs of struggle. Whatever had happened here had happened to someone who hadn't understood it was happening until it was past preventing.

Like the jury itself, she thought. Like everyone

who Morrison had needed to not quite see what he was doing.

She found the number on the wall behind the chair without having to search for it — carved into the plaster with the same clean precision as all the others.

Eight. Eight victims now. Eight days. The sequence was accelerating, or she was losing track at the edges, or both. "Why not inform us after his murder?" She asked again. "If he's been dead for two days…"

"He should've been number six," Trevor said. "He's messing with us.

She looked at the sheep one more time, at the flock scattered around a man who had almost understood something important and had paid for the almost as surely as he would have paid for the full understanding. *He wanted us to believe something.*

The jury had been guided. Not coerced. They had been led somewhere they thought they were choosing to go.

That was the most complete kind of control. The kind the subject never feels.

They processed the scene and drove back to the station in relative quiet, the sunlight stronger now, the morning fully committed to its own clarity. Shea sat in the passenger seat and watched the town move past and turned the sequence over in her mind, looking for the next piece, the next name, the next nursery rhyme already being prepared somewhere she hadn't found yet.

Back in the bullpen, she stood at the board for a long time without speaking. Trevor came to stand beside her — not crowding, just present, the way he had been present all week.

"Eight," she said.

"Yes."

"Morrison." She said the name the way she always said it now — not as a question, not as an accusation, just as the fact at the center of everything. "Every victim traces back to him. Every role, every nursery rhyme, every piece of the sequence. He's the point of origin, and he's going to be the end of it."

The bullpen had quieted around them. Snelling and Webster worked at their desks. It felt, for a moment, like a pocket of stillness inside the ongoing motion of the day.

Trevor turned to face her fully, and she recognized something in his expression that she had been catching at the edges of all week. Something present, patient, and waiting for a moment that wasn't entirely consumed by the case.

"Come here," he said quietly.

It wasn't a request she expected. She looked at him.

He crossed the small distance between them and put his arms around her in the embrace of someone who had decided this was necessary and wasn't going to apologize for the decision. She felt his hand at the back of her head, the solid warmth of him, and something in her chest that had been drawn taut for eight days released in a way that surprised her with its completeness.

She didn't pull away. For a moment, she just stood there, her forehead against his shoulder, her hands finding the fabric of his jacket, and let the weight of it exist without trying to manage it. Eight days of bodies and patterns and the relentless pressure of being three steps behind someone who planned everything. Eight days of holding the shape of the investigation together through force of will, of being the one people looked at when they needed to know the next move. She let herself not know the next move for thirty seconds.

His thumb moved once, slowly, at the back of her neck. "You're not behind," he said quietly, against her hair. "You're exactly where you need to be."

She didn't answer immediately. She was aware of Snelling and Webster at their desks, of the ordinary sounds of the station around them, and found she didn't particularly care about any of it.

"He has more names," she said finally. "Including mine."

"Then we find him before he gets to them…to you."

She stepped back. His hand fell from her shoulder slowly. She looked at him for a moment. "Thank you."

He nodded once. Simple. Uncomplicated. "I'm coming over tonight, and I'm going to bring the most boring movie I can find so you'll sleep." He gave a lopsided smile.

She returned his smile, then turned back to the board. "Pull Morrison's current associates," she said, her voice back in its working register, clean and directed. "Not historical. Current. Anyone he's been in contact with in the past six months — phone, financial, in person." She looked at Snelling. "And cross-reference with every remaining name on the unaccounted roster. "

"On it," Snelling said.

Outside, the sun continued its uncomplicated work across Misty Hollow, laying clean light over a town that deserved better than what had happened inside it this week.

She intended to give it that.

Chapter Eleven

Shea was already awake when her phone lit up on the nightstand. She saw his name and felt the tightening in her chest before she answered.

"Where?" No greeting. No preamble. Nine days in, they had shed everything that wasn't necessary.

"Old rail yard off Miller Road. Patrol found an abandoned vehicle. There's blood." Trevor paused. "Shea, this one's different."

Her hand had already found her jacket on the chair beside the bed. "How?"

"He didn't finish clean."

She was out the door in four minutes.

The sky was the deep blue-gray of predawn, and the unusually cold air for March was cold enough that her breath showed as she stepped out of her vehicle onto the gravel road leading into the rail yard. The place had been dormant for years — rusted equipment, sections of track reclaimed slowly by weeds pushing through fractured concrete. The kind of place that existed in the negative space of a town's attention.

Trevor's truck sat parked at an angle near a dark sedan with the driver's door hanging open.

He met her halfway across the gravel, his expression carrying something she hadn't seen on him in nine days of this. Not just the controlled gravity he brought to every scene. Something tighter than that.

"Walk me through it," she said.

"Blood in the driver's seat. Significant amount." He turned and pointed toward the tracks. "Trail leads that direction. It's not straight."

Snelling and Webster already worked the perimeter, moving along the edge of the tracks in the gray light, their flashlights cutting low across the ground. Shea followed Trevor toward them, her eyes adjusting, and then she saw it.

The blood trail was wrong.

Not wrong in the way the other scenes had been wrong. This was wrong in the way of panic. The drops staggered, spacing uneven and smeared in places where someone had gone down and then pushed themselves up again or been pushed. The gravel was disturbed in arcs that suggested movement without direction, someone trying to find a way through something rather than moving toward anything.

She crouched near a concentration of drops and studied the pattern. "He fought."

Trevor stopped beside her. "Hard from the look of it."

"Not at the end. Throughout." She stood. "Someone knew what was coming and didn't go quietly."

That was new. Whoever had died here had not been sedated first. Or had been, and it hadn't held.

They followed the trail further along the tracks, the air colder in the open stretch, the sound of the town completely absent out here. The ground dipped, and then the body came into view.

He lay partially on his side just beyond the rail line, one arm extended in front of him, palm down against the gravel, fingers spread in the posture of someone who had been trying to move and hadn't made it. His clothing was torn at the shoulder. Abrasions on the side of his face. No nursery rhyme staging. No careful arrangement. No carved number on any surface nearby.

Just an ending, unfinished and exposed.

Shea stood over him and let the absence of the usual ritual settle into meaning. This hadn't been planned as it was. Something, or someone, had interrupted the sequence. The result was a scene that was more honest than anything they'd found in nine days — the actual mechanics of what this was, stripped of the presentation that had been layered over every other victim.

"ID?" she asked.

"In the vehicle," Trevor said. "Alan Mercer. Licensed private investigator out of the county."

The name registered immediately. "He worked the Morrison case."

Snelling looked at her. "You knew him?"

"Not personally. He was hired by the defense. He's in the original case file. Ran background investigation on Jennifer, dug into her history, produced the character analysis that helped undermine her credibility during the trial." She paused. "He was good at his job."

"Good enough to figure something out afterward," Webster said.

"Apparently." She looked at Mercer — at the extended hand, the torn shoulder, the face turned into the gravel — and felt the particular weight of a man who had spent years being useful to the wrong people and had then, at some point in the intervening years, looked clearly at what he had been useful for.

Then she saw the notebook tucked partially under his outstretched hand, the cover dark, the pages curled. She crouched and pulled on gloves before moving his hand carefully aside. She opened it.

The pages were dense. Overlapping entries, dates crowded into margins, arrows connecting names across pages as if the writer had been moving faster than the notebook could accommodate, chasing something that kept expanding as he got closer to it. She flipped through it, reading as she went.

Names she recognized. Dates that aligned with the trial. And then, deeper in, something that made her slow down.

Adjusted responses before cross-examination. Anticipated questions he should not have known. Someone inside the process.

She turned another page.

Document transfers — defense to chambers. Not standard routing. Three instances confirmed, two suspected.

Another page.

He is not reacting to the trial. He is directing it.

She stopped there. "Mercer knew."

Trevor leaned in slightly. She held the notebook at an angle so he could read the line. His jaw tightened. "How long had he been working on this?"

"Since the trial, I'm guessing." She turned more pages, her eyes moving quickly, catching names and dates and connections that were going to take hours to fully parse. The notebook was a map of someone's slow and private revelation — a man who had done work he hadn't fully understood at the time and had spent years afterward following the implications of it back to their source.

Then she reached the back section. A list.

Names in a column, each one with a date beside it and a small mark of something checked off. She felt her stomach drop before she fully processed what she was reading.

Lila Vance. Evelyn Hart. Megan Doyle. Harold Briggs. Carol Finch. Daniel Reeves. Richard Hale. Laura Bennett. Daniel Pierce. Every victim, in order, with the date of their death beside their name.

And at the bottom of the column, below the last checked entry, two names remained.

The first was Morrison. The second was hers. *Callahan. Written next to his, not on a line underneath.* No date yet.

No mark. Just the name.

She stared at it for a long moment. The cold air moved across the tracks, pulling at her jacket, and the world reduced itself briefly to the page in her hands.

"Shea." Trevor's voice was quiet.

She turned the notebook toward him without speaking. She watched him find it. Watched his expression move through recognition and then through something more controlled and deliberate, the way he managed responses that he wasn't going to let become reactions.

Webster had moved closer. Snelling too. She didn't try to soften it.

"He has a sequence," she said. "Mercer had documented it — either he found it, or he compiled it from what he knew, or both. Morrison is the second-to-last name." She looked at the notebook, at her own name in someone else's handwriting. "He intends to take his own life and me with him."

Webster said, "We move you to—"

"No," she said. "I'm the final piece. The last person to fail. I have to see this through." An icy fist gripped her heart.

Trevor looked at her. The expression on his face was the one he used when he was deciding how hard to push something. "You need to hear what comes after no."

"I know what comes after it," she said. "Protection detail, reduced exposure, someone else running point. And I'm telling you that's not how this ends."

"He has your name on a kill list." Trevor's voice rose barely above a growl. "In a notebook held by a man who figured out the sequence and is now dead on a gravel road."

"I know."

"Then act like it."

She met his eyes. "I am acting like it. Acting like it means I stay in this until it's finished, because the moment I step back is the moment he adjusts and we lose the thread we've been building for nine days." She looked at the notebook. "He left me for last for a reason. He's been watching this investigation. He knows my involvement. Which means he's been close enough to observe…and that proximity is something we can use."

"Or something he's already using," Snelling said carefully.

"Yes." Shea nodded. "Both things are true."

Trevor hadn't looked away from her. She could feel the weight of what he wasn't saying — the things that existed between them in the margins of the professional, the things that a week and a half of shared pressure had made impossible to entirely ignore. She held his gaze steadily. "I won't be reckless."

"That's not the same as safe."

"No," she agreed. "It isn't."

He looked at her for a long moment. Then he exhaled. "Then you don't go anywhere alone," he said. "Not the station, not the field, not home. That's not negotiable. I'll pack a few of my things after work."

She held his gaze. "Agreed."

His hand came to her arm, just above the elbow, and stayed there. Not the brief grounding contact of the past nine days. Something more deliberate. His thumb pressed once against the fabric of her jacket, a small and certain gesture that said several things he wasn't going to say out loud in a crime scene with their team ten feet away.

She put her hand over his briefly. Just that. Just the acknowledgment.

Then she looked back at the scene, at Mercer, at the broken trail across the gravel. "He didn't get to stage this. Which tells us something important. Mercer disrupted him. Got close enough with what he knew to force a response that wasn't planned, wasn't careful, wasn't controlled." She glanced back at the notebook. "Which means the careful, controlled version of Morrison is starting to have edges."

"Pressure points," Snelling said.

"Yes. He's been operating from a position of total preparedness for nine days. Mercer introduced a variable he hadn't fully accounted for, and the result is this — the first scene that looks like something went wrong." She turned the notebook over in her hands. "We find out everything Mercer knew. Who he talked to, what he'd confirmed, what he was about to confirm. Because whatever got him killed is the same thing that could end this."

Webster turned, his phone to his ear. Snelling started photographing the notebook pages.

Trevor stayed beside her as she did one final slow survey of the scene — the body, the trail, the abandoned car with its door still open to the cold morning air. The sky had fully committed to dawn now, the flat gray yielding to something warmer, the sun arriving without ceremony over the tree line to the east and laying itself across the rail yard and everything in it.

"He thinks I'm the end of this," she said quietly.

Trevor cut her a sideways glance.

"He's wrong," she said.

She marched toward the vehicles, the gravel shifting under her boots, the cold morning air carrying the smell of rust and wet earth, and the very ordinary world continuing its business around a crime scene at the edge of a town that deserved to stop finding bodies.

Her name, last on a list.

It didn't surprise her that he had been watching her since the beginning. Had factored her into the sequence not as an obstacle but as a component. She had been the arresting officer to his crime. Testified at his trial.

She stopped at her vehicle and turned back to look at the rail yard, at the tracks and the rusted equipment and the place where a man had died holding the evidence of what he'd finally understood.

Trevor caught up to her.

She got in the car and started the engine, and the morning opened up in front of her, and somewhere in Misty Hollow, the man whose name was second-to-last on that list was already moving toward whatever he had always intended to be the end.

She intended to get there first.

Chapter Twelve

Shea didn't go home.

Not after the rail yard. Not after seeing her name written in a dead man's notebook at the bottom of a list where everyone above it was already gone. The station was the only place that felt even partially contained, and even that was becoming harder to believe with each hour that passed.

By mid-afternoon, the sky outside had gone clear and pale, the sun dropping toward the tree line. Inside, the bullpen carried a tension that had changed quality — quieter, more deliberate.

Shea stood at the case board. Nine victims now, counting Mercer, and she did count him. Whether Morrison had intended the investigator's death to be part of the sequence or had been forced into it by circumstance didn't change what it was. Mercer had understood something, had gotten close enough to document it, and had died for the proximity. That made him part of this regardless of whether the scene fit the pattern.

And at the bottom of the list in Mercer's notebook, below nine names with dates and marks beside them — Her name.

Trevor stood a few feet behind her. He had been doing that since the rail yard, staying within range without pressing into her space, close enough to be felt without being intrusive. She had stopped noticing it consciously and started relying on it unconsciously, which was its own kind of information about where things stood between them.

"You're trying to outthink him from inside the pattern," he said.

"I'm trying to find what we're missing."

"We're not missing anything obvious."

"That's been true since day one and hasn't slowed him down once," she said.

He didn't argue. He knew she was right.

Snelling and Webster came into the bullpen together, both carrying folders, both wearing the expression of people who had found something significant and were calculating how to present it.

"Mercer's off-site storage." Snelling set the folder on the desk and opened it without preamble. "Encrypted files buried under unrelated case work. He didn't just have suspicions, Shea. He was building a case over what looks like the better part of two years."

Webster spread several printed documents across the surface. "He was thorough. Cross-referenced. Some of this is going to take forensic accounting to fully parse, but the outline is legible."

Shea moved to the desk and started reading. The documents were dense. Timelines with annotations. Names connected by arrows across multiple pages. Financial records with specific transactions circled. And threaded through all of it, returning again and again, the architecture of the Morrison trial laid out not as it had appeared publicly but as it had actually functioned.

She turned a page and stopped. "Prosecution strategy notes."

Trevor stepped beside her. "From the trial?"

"Yes." She read the section quickly. "These aren't official documents. They're reconstructed. Mercer built them from cross-referencing depositions, court transcripts, and communications he'd obtained somewhere along the way." She turned another page. "He was tracking specific moments where the prosecution's case lost structural integrity."

Snelling pointed to a circled section near the bottom of the page. "He notes the same three witnesses. Each one had their credibility challenged before they testified — not during cross-examination, but before. Their histories surfaced in ways that undercut their value before they'd said a word."

Webster added, "And each time, the information appeared to come from public sources. Completely legitimate on the surface."

"Because he made it look that way." Shea flipped to the next section. "He didn't just work the defense. He was working the prosecution simultaneously. Feeding information that looked like due diligence and was actually sabotage. Making the prosecution's own strategy the mechanism of its failure."

The room went quiet.

Trevor said, "He was on both sides of the table."

Shea nodded. "The defense did what defenses do — built the best case they could with what they had. The prosecution did the same. But the information both of them were working from had been shaped in advance. The prosecution thought they were responding to reality. They were responding to a version of reality he had constructed for them."

Snelling exhaled slowly. "So, when the case fell apart—"

"It looked like the system failing," Shea said. "Procedural errors, weak evidence, witnesses who didn't hold up. All of it explicable, none of it traceable back to a single point of interference, because there wasn't a single point. There were dozens. Distributed across months. Built into the foundation before the first day of trial."

Webster shook his head slightly. "That's a level of preparation that goes far beyond a man trying to avoid a conviction."

"Yes," she said. "It does, but Morrison didn't want to avoid a conviction. He wanted to be punished for what he did. He's been playing a game the whole time to see whether we can take him down."

Before anyone could follow that further, the radio crackled.

Unit three — possible DOA at a residence on Pemberton. Victim found in her home office. Caller is a colleague who came for a scheduled meeting. Scene appears staged.

The house sat in a quiet neighborhood of well-maintained properties. The victim's home fit its surroundings: substantial without excess, professional in the way it presented itself, a place that said its owner had built a life from discipline and consistency.

The front door stood open. Lights on inside. A patrol officer at the threshold with the careful stillness of someone maintaining composure through deliberate effort.

"She's in the office," he said. "Back of the house."

The interior was ordered with bookshelves arranged with intention, furniture placed with the awareness of someone who thought about how spaces functioned. The smell reached Shea halfway down the hall. Sweet, faint, chemical underneath. She knew it now the way she knew the sound of her own voice.

The office doorway framed the scene before she stepped through it. The victim sat behind her desk in the upright posture of someone interrupted mid-task. Her hands rested palms-down on the desk surface. Her head tilted slightly to the right, expression neutral, eyes closed. She could have been thinking.

Across the desk, arranged in a careful arc in front of her folded hands were coins. Silver and dull, stacked in small deliberate columns that had clearly been placed rather than spilled. Six stacks, each one the same height, the whole arrangement symmetrical in a way that natural distribution never produced.

"Sing a song of sixpence," Shea said quietly.

Trevor stepped in behind her. "A pocket full of rye."

Snelling moved to the side of the desk, her eyes traveling the arrangement. "Four and twenty blackbirds."

"Baked in a pie," Webster finished, his voice flat.

The nursery rhyme settled into the room and Shea let it, working the meaning the way she had learned to work all of them.

A pocket full of rye. Wealth. Sufficiency. The accumulation of something that should have been used differently. The coins on the desk weren't payment — they were accounting. An inventory of what this woman had possessed and how she had spent it.

She had been the prosecutor. She had held the weight of the case in her hands, and it had dissolved, piece by piece, through failures that had looked like her own inadequacy and had been engineered from the outside.

He was putting the coins back on her desk. Showing her account.

Shea moved around the perimeter of the room, reading the space, and found the number on the wall behind the desk without having to search for it. Carved into the plaster with the same clean instrument as every other mark in this sequence.

Nine.

She stood and looked at it for a moment.

Nine days. Nine deaths. Her name still at the bottom of a list with one entry above it. Mercer's death hadn't been planned.

"She ran the prosecution." Trevor read from his phone. "Lead ADA. Assigned eight months before trial, replaced at the last minute due to what was reported as a family emergency."

Shea turned. "Replaced by whom?"

Trevor scrolled. "Junior ADA named Garrett Holt. No prior experience with cases of this complexity." He paused. "He's the one who argued the trial."

"And lost it," Snelling said.

"Because someone made sure the senior prosecutor wasn't in the room." Shea studied the victim. The coins arranged on the desk and the careful staging of a woman who had been removed from her own case before she could be a problem. "She didn't fail. She was replaced. And whoever replaced her was either incompetent or complicit."

"Which one?" Webster asked.

"I don't know yet," she said. "But I want Holt found and brought in today."

She looked back at the laptop on the corner of the desk. Open, screen dark, positioned in a way that felt deliberate — not how you left a computer when you were interrupted, but how you placed one when you wanted it found.

She pressed a key. The screen came up immediately, no sleep delay, as if it had been waiting.

A document filled the screen. Not the victim's work. The formatting was wrong, the font was different from the documents stacked beside the keyboard, and the margins were set in a way that no one would configure for professional use. It had been placed here, opened, and left for whoever arrived.

She leaned in and read. The document was a prosecution strategy outline — detailed, structured, reading at first glance like the kind of internal case preparation document that would be standard in any serious trial. But the margins were annotated in a different hand, dense with notes that tracked the outline's arguments and, beside each one, a notation.

Weakened — medical records surfaced D-14.

Witness withdrawn — prior statement obtained D-22.

Argument undermined — procedural challenge filed D-9.

Dates before the trial. Interventions timed to specific moments in the prosecution's preparation. Each one landed at a point where the argument was still being built, where the damage could be absorbed into the structure rather than appearing as an external attack.

"He left this for us," Trevor said.

"Yes." She straightened. "He's been leaving things for us since the beginning — the scenes, the symbols, the calls. This is different. This is the mechanism. He's showing us how it was done."

Snelling's voice was careful. "Why would he do that now?"

Shea looked at the document, at the annotated evidence of a trial that had been choreographed from the inside out and understood with sudden clarity what had changed.

"Because we're reaching the end," she said. "He's not hiding the method anymore because hiding it no longer serves him. He wants us to see the full scope of what he built before—" She stopped.

Before it concluded, she had been about to say. Before he gets to the last two names on the list.

Trevor was watching her. He had heard the pause and understood it.

"Get everything off that laptop." She turned to Webster, keeping her voice even. "Full forensic extraction. I want metadata, access history, when that document was placed, and from what device." She looked at Snelling. "And pull everything on Garrett Holt, the replacement ADA. Financial records, communications, any connection to Morrison or his defense team going back five years before the trial."

She took one more look at the ADA behind her

desk — at the coins, at the careful stillness, at the life of a woman whose competence had been removed from the equation precisely because it was competence.

"He didn't lose the prosecution," she said quietly. "He excised it."

Then she marched out of the room and down the hallway, and stood for a moment in the front doorway, the late-afternoon light coming flat and golden across the street outside, the neighborhood completely ordinary around the edges of what had happened inside this house.

Trevor appeared at her shoulder. "You're seeing the whole board now."

"Most of it anyway."

"What's the part you don't have yet?"

She thought about the notebook, about her name at the bottom, about the second-to-last name above it. "Morrison knows we're close. Mercer got close, and Morrison responded — badly, rushed, out of sequence. That's not a man operating from a position of comfort anymore." She paused. "Which means he's making decisions under pressure for the first time in this entire case."

"And pressure creates mistakes," Trevor said.

"Yes." She turned to peer up at him. "We just have to make sure I'm not one of them."

He held her gaze for a moment — long enough that what passed between them was more than professional, what it had been for days without either of them naming it, the accumulated weight of nine days of proximity and shared horror and the specific intimacy of working at the edge of something dangerous with someone you trusted completely.

"You won't be," he said.

His hand came to the side of her face. Briefly, just his fingers against her jaw, the gentlest possible contact, the kind that asked nothing and said everything. She let herself feel it fully for the three seconds it lasted before he lowered his hand and they both returned to the work, because the work was what remained, and they both understood that.

She returned to the vehicle in the long golden light of a day that was running out, and behind her, the house sat quiet with its coins and its careful staging, and its document left open on a screen like a confession from someone who had decided the time for concealment had passed.

He was finishing the design. She could feel it closing around her like weather.

She intended to be standing when it broke.

Chapter Thirteen

Shea stood just inside the doorway of the evidence room and let her eyes adjust.

Rows of shelving extended in careful lines, each unit labeled in the station's standard system, each box cataloged and positioned with the order of a room that no one ever rushed through. Evidence rooms rewarded patience. They were organized around the principle that everything here mattered, that nothing should be touched without reason, that the chain of custody was the integrity of the case, and the integrity of the case was everything.

At the far end of the room, a deputy stood with one hand resting on the edge of a shelf, his posture carrying the mood of someone trying to project steadiness and not quite managing it.

Trevor stepped in behind her. "She was found by the morning shift?"

"Overnight clerk called it in," the deputy said. "She was doing a late inventory check. Alone."

Shea moved forward.

The body came into view between two rows of shelving. Karen Ellis, evidence clerk. She lay on her side with one arm bent beneath her, head turned toward the unit beside her, her expression frozen in surprise. The boxes on the nearest shelf had been pulled slightly out of alignment. Not toppled, not scattered, just shifted with a few inches of displacement that was enough to partially obscure the body without suggesting any kind of struggle.

She had been tucked in. That was the only way to describe it. Placed among the evidence with the same deliberate attention as every scene before this one.

Snelling crouched at the perimeter, her gaze moving through the scene. Webster stood to the side, scanning the upper shelving units.

"No signs of struggle anywhere else in the room," Webster said. "Nothing disturbed except those two boxes."

"He moved them after," Snelling said. "Not before."

Shea pulled on gloves and crouched beside the victim, studying the positioning. The arm beneath the body would have been placed that way. It didn't reflect how someone fell. The angle of the head was too specific, too considered. And the expression, frozen in interrupted surprise rather than fear, suggested she hadn't understood what was happening until the moment it happened.

Fast. Controlled. Someone she didn't perceive as a threat, or didn't perceive at all, until it was past the point of reaction.

"Did she have reason to be looking at anything specific tonight?" Shea asked the deputy.

"Annual reconciliation," he said. "We run it every quarter. She was checking physical evidence against the digital logs — confirming everything is where the system says it is."

Shea stood slowly. She studied the shelves around the body. At the boxes, at the labels, and at the section of the room where Karen Ellis had been working when she was interrupted. Her gaze moved along the row until it stopped on a file box sitting slightly ajar, its lid resting at an angle that was too precise to be accidental. If the lid had simply been displaced, it would have fallen. Someone had positioned it to stay open. To be noticed.

"Don't touch anything else." She crossed to the box and lifted the lid carefully.

Inside — files. Old ones, the kind with the worn edges and faded ink of documents that had been handled multiple times and then put away and not touched again. The labels were partially obscured by age, but legible.

Morrison's case files.

She felt Trevor's presence close behind her as she pulled the first file free. Evidence logs. Chain-of-custody reports. Inventory records from the original case, the physical documentation of every piece of evidence that had been collected, processed, and submitted in the trial that had defined the past decade of this town's relationship with its own institutions.

She opened it. Read the first page. Then turned to the second. Something didn't align.

She went back to the first page and read more carefully, cross-referencing the two documents side by side, her pulse picking up as the discrepancy resolved into clarity. "These records don't match."

Trevor stepped in beside her. "What do you mean?"

"The same evidence." She held both pages toward him. "Same case number, same item description, same collection date. Logged twice. Once as submitted and complete, once as incomplete, pending verification." She looked at him. "On the same day."

Trevor's eyes moved across the pages. "That's a clerical error."

"No," she said. "Look at the authorizing signatures."

He looked. She watched his expression shift. "Different people."

"Different people. Same day. Same evidence. One version says it's there. One says it isn't." She set the pages on the shelf carefully and turned to Snelling. "We need to pull every evidence log from the Morrison trial — physical copies, not the digital system. Whatever's in this room, not what the computer says is in this room."

Snelling nodded and moved.

Webster stepped closer, looking at the open file. "If the records were intentionally falsified—"

"The evidence chain fails," Trevor said.

"Which means anything dependent on that evidence becomes inadmissible," Shea said. "Not because the evidence was bad. Because the paperwork around it was compromised in a specific, targeted way that created enough procedural uncertainty to challenge the whole chain."

She looked at the box, at the files, at the Morrison case documentation sitting in an evidence room in the station where the investigation into the Morrison murders was currently being run. "He put this here."

Webster frowned. "How? When?"

"Not tonight. This documentation has been here for years. It's part of the original case archive." She closed the file carefully. "He didn't plant it recently. He planted it before the trial. Knowing it would sit here, undiscovered, part of the official record, until someone looked at it closely enough."

"And Karen Ellis looked at it closely enough," Trevor said.

"During a routine inventory check." Shea looked at the body. "She wasn't a target in the sequence. She wasn't on his list of people who shaped the Morrison trial's outcome. She was collateral damage. Someone who found the wrong thing at the wrong time and had to be dealt with before she reported it."

Snelling glanced up from where she worked through a second box further down the row. "Then this is different from the others."

"Yes and no," Shea said. "The method is the same. The care is the same. But the reason isn't about the trial anymore. It's about protecting the evidence of the trial's manipulation from being discovered before he's ready for it to be discovered." She paused. "He has a timeline. He's been executing it for ten days without deviation. Karen Ellis threatened that timeline, and he responded."

"Which means he's been watching the station," Webster said.

The statement landed, and no one immediately moved past it.

"He knew she was doing an inventory check tonight," Shea said. "He knew she was working alone. He knew which section she'd reach and when." She looked at the deputy. "Who schedules the inventory rotations?"

"It's posted on the internal system," the deputy said.

"So anyone with access to department records would have it."

"Yes, ma'am."

Trevor exhaled quietly. "He's inside our systems."

"He's been inside everything from the beginning," Shea said, her rate racing. Morrison stayed two steps ahead of them, and time was ticking down to her name on the list. "We keep finding that out one piece at a time." She pulled out her phone and photographed both pages of the evidence log before returning them to the box. "I want a full audit of station system access over the past thirty days. Every login, every record retrieval, every query that touches the Morrison case files."

Webster moved immediately toward the door to start the request.

Snelling still worked through the second box and had gone very still.

"What is it?" Shea asked.

"Come look at this."

Shea crossed the room. Snelling had a different file open — newer than the Morrison originals, the paper less yellowed, the formatting slightly different. She held it toward Shea without comment.

It was an inventory reconciliation. Recent — dated three weeks ago. A routine quarterly check, the same process Karen Ellis had been conducting tonight. The clerk who had signed it was someone else, a name Shea recognized as a former employee who had retired eighteen months prior. Except that the check had been conducted three weeks ago.

"He signed it," Shea said.

"His name is on it," Snelling said. "That's not the same as him signing it."

Shea looked at the document. At the falsified signature, at the date, at the reconciliation entries that would have shown everything in order and directed attention away from exactly the discrepancies Karen Ellis had found tonight. Someone had conducted a fraudulent inventory check three weeks ago, specifically to create a clean record that would make the real anomalies harder to find.

"He was clearing the path," she said. "Making sure the falsified evidence logs wouldn't surface accidentally during the normal rotation. But the normal rotation still happened — just ahead of schedule, when he could control who signed off on it." She handed the document back to Snelling. "He knew we'd get here eventually. He just needed us to get here on his timeline, not ours."

She turned and found the number without looking for it. It was on the edge of the metal shelving unit, at eye level, in the same clean incised line as every other mark in this sequence. Not the wall this time — the shelf itself, the infrastructure of the room, the structure that held everything together.

Ten.

She stood in front of it and counted backward. Ten victims. Herself at the bottom of the list. One name above hers. Morrison.

Trevor appeared beside her, and she felt him look at the number and then at her, reading her reaction. "Ten."

""Mercer was unplanned — rushed, out of sequence. I think I discounted it as a clean entry in the count." She kept her eyes on the carved number. "He counted it. Everybody is a step in the sequence, planned or improvised, and he's keeping the count. Which means he knows exactly where he is and exactly what remains."

The evidence room was quiet around them, the shelves full of other people's stories, the overhead lights casting the same dim, even light across everything. Somewhere between the rows, Karen Ellis lay where she had been placed, a woman whose only connection to any of this had been the unlucky intersection of a routine task and a document that wasn't supposed to be found yet.

Trevor's hand came to her back, steady and full. She didn't move away.

"He's running out of names," he said quietly.

"Four left," she said. "Morrison and then me. He's been working toward this for ten years and days before that." She paused. "He's not going to stop. Not because of evidence, not because we're close, not because we understand the design. He'll stop when it's finished or when we stop him."

"Then we stop him."

They kept saying that, but were gaining very little ground. She turned to face him.

Up close in the dim light of the evidence room, she could see the cost of ten days on him, too. The lines that hadn't been there before the first body, the quality of attention that came from sustained vigilance, the particular steadiness of someone who had been holding something together through force of character and hadn't let it slip once.

"When this is over," she said.

He looked at her. Waited.

"We're going to go away," she said. "Just the two of us. Get away from this town for a few days."

Something shifted in his expression — not surprise, not the performance of casualness. Just the quiet acknowledgment of something that had been true for a while, finding its first words.

"Yes," he said. "I'd like that."

She held his gaze for a moment. Then she turned back to the room, to the work, to the ten steps of a sequence that had only a few remaining.

"Full audit on system access," she said to Snelling, her voice back in its working register. "Physical evidence log reconciliation against the digital system for every Morrison file. And I want Garrett Holt, the replacement ADA, brought in today. Not requested. Brought."

She walked out of the evidence room into the lit hallway of the station that someone had been inside, had accessed, had used as part of the design of something that was now entering its final stage.

Ten down.

Four remaining.

Then Morrison. The other was her.

Chapter Fourteen

The station didn't feel safe anymore. That realization had been building for days. Standing in the hallway outside the evidence room, the door closed behind her, Shea let it settle fully for the first time.

He had been inside this building. Had accessed their systems, had known about Karen Ellis's inventory rotation, had moved through the station as easily as he moved through everything else he had built and rebuilt over the past decade. The investigation into his crimes was being run from a building he had already been inside.

"He adjusted," Trevor said beside her.

"He didn't adjust." She turned from the door. "He planned for this. He needed us to find the evidence logs. Needed us to see the falsification, to understand that the trial's failure wasn't incompetence. Everything we're finding, we're finding on his timeline."

Trevor was quiet for a moment, reading her. "Then he's still directing it."

"Yes." She held his gaze. "But the direction is changing. We're not just following the sequence anymore, Trevor. We're being positioned inside it."

Snelling appeared at the far end of the hallway, her expression grave. "We've got something. West side, residential. Uniform found a scene. Not a body yet, but it's not right."

Not a body yet.

"Let's go," Shea said.

The street was the kind of ordinary that made everything feel more wrong — a narrow residential block with modest houses. The kind of neighborhood where people knew each other by name and left porch lights on. Two patrol cars sat at the curb with their lights off, engines running, the officers standing back from the front porch.

The front door of the house stood open.

Trevor moved ahead slightly. "What do we have?"

The nearest officer stepped forward. "Neighbor called it in. Said she heard arguing, then it stopped suddenly. When she looked out, the front door was open, and nobody came out."

"How long ago?" Shea asked.

"Thirty minutes."

"Why is no one inside?"

The officer hesitated. "There's something written on the wall. Dispatch told us to hold for you."

Shea looked at the open door. The darkness of the interior beyond it, the curtains drawn on either side of the frame, the complete stillness of a house that should have had someone in it.

Trevor stepped into her line of sight. Not blocking her — positioning himself. "Together," he said. It wasn't a question.

She nodded.

He went through the door first, her half a step behind and to his left, both of them reading the room as it resolved from darkness into detail. The interior was ordinary with furniture in place, nothing overturned, no signs of the kind of disturbance that announced itself. The smell was faint and warm and chemical underneath, familiar in a way that tightened something in her chest before she had consciously identified it.

Then she saw the wall.

Across the far side of the living room, in dark uneven strokes, applied with something that had bled slightly at the edges:

THIS LITTLE PIGGY WENT TO MARKET

Webster's voice from behind her, quiet. "It's different."

"Yes," she said.

Different in its directness. Every other scene had allowed the nursery rhyme to emerge from the physical staging — the wool in the grass, the ceramic fragments on the courthouse steps, the hanging cradle. This one announced itself. The words on the wall were the scene, presented without the staging around them. More urgent. Less controlled.

Or controlled differently. She wasn't sure yet.

"Clear the house," she ordered.

Officers moved through the rooms quickly, calling out as they went — kitchen, bathroom, back room, all clear — until one voice in the rear of the house faltered in the middle of a word.

The silence that followed lasted less than two seconds. "Victim found. Bedroom."

Shea rushed down the hall, Trevor right behind her.

The bedroom was small, simply furnished, the overhead light on and casting everything in flat, even brightness. The victim lay on the bed — positioned, Shea saw immediately, with the deliberate care that had characterized every staged scene in this sequence. But this one was different in the way that mattered most.

Her chest was rising and falling. Shallow, uneven. But present.

For a fraction of a second, Shea's mind refused to recalibrate — ten days of bodies, of stillness, of the specific finality that had defined every scene — and then it did, and she was across the room.

"EMS," Trevor said sharply behind her. "Now."

Snelling had the woman's wrist, fingers on her pulse. "Weak, but there. Sedated."

The woman's hands were bound loosely at the wrists with the kind of restraint that held without cutting off circulation, the kind applied by someone who needed her contained but not damaged. Her skin was pale and cool. Her breathing had the shallow, effortful quality of someone fighting through heavy sedation.

Shea did a rapid scan of the room. No other staging beyond positioning; no coins, figurines, or symbolic objects. No nursery rhyme continuation beyond what was written in the other room.

Then she found the number. On the wall beside the headboard, at the height of someone seated on the bed, carved into the paint with the same clean instrument as every other mark in this sequence.

Ten.

She stared at it.

Not nine. Ten.

Which meant her count had been wrong, or the sequence had accelerated, or both. She worked it backward quickly — Vance, Hart, Doyle, Briggs, Finch, Reeves, Hale, Bennett, Price, Ellis. Ten names, some planned, some improvised, all counted. And this woman still breathing.

"Ten," Trevor said quietly beside her. "But she's alive."

"He didn't finish," Shea said.

"Or he chose not to."

She looked at the woman on the bed. A juror, she was already certain. The logic of the sequence demanded it, another person who had sat in that courtroom and participated in the outcome, another role in the story Morrison had written. But alive. Left alive deliberately, in a house with the front door open, in a neighborhood where a concerned neighbor would call within thirty minutes.

"He wanted us to find her like this," she said.

Trevor looked at her. "Before she died."

"Yes."

"Why?"

She turned it over, working the logic from his perspective rather than hers. Every scene had been a communication. Not just a killing but a message, each one building on the one before it, each nursery rhyme a piece of the larger text he had been composing since the first body. This was a different kind of message. Not completion. Demonstration.

"He's showing us he has control over the ending," she said. "Not just the sequence, but also the outcome. He can choose whether they live or die. He's been killing everyone on the list, and now he's left one alive, and he needs us to understand that the difference between those two things is his choice." She paused. "He's reminding us that nothing that happens from here is accidental. Everything is exactly what he decides it to be."

Including whatever came next.

Webster had moved to the window, scanning the yard beyond. "No sign of exit. Ground's soft enough to show prints, but there's nothing."

"He's still close," Snelling said.

The quality of the room changed.

Not in any physical way — the same light, the same space, the same woman breathing on the bed. But the awareness that the distance between themselves and Morrison had collapsed from theoretical to immediate moved through the room like a current.

Shea felt it in her spine.

Trevor felt it too. She saw it in the way he shifted, his body orienting slightly toward the doorway, toward the rest of the house, toward wherever the sound that didn't belong might come from.

A floorboard creaked.

The sound was small and definite, and every person in the room went completely still.

Trevor's hand moved to his weapon without drama, a single deliberate motion.

Webster mouthed: *Back of the house.*

They moved together — Trevor leading, Shea behind him and to the left, Snelling and Webster spreading to cover the width of the hallway as they made their way toward the rear of the house. Each step was placed with care. The house smaller in this mode, every shadow carrying potential.

The door at the end of the hall stood slightly ajar.

Trevor pushed it open with his foot, weapon raised, scanning left and right. Empty.

But the window on the far wall was open, the curtains lifting and settling in the breeze coming through, and the cold, fresh air was a statement. He had been in this room, had left through this window, had heard them arrive, and made a decision.

Trevor crossed to the window and looked out, scanning the yard in both directions. "Nothing."

Of course.

Shea moved into the room, scanning the surfaces, the floor, the window frame itself. She found it before she had fully processed the instinct to look — on the inside of the window frame, at shoulder height, carved into the wood with fresh edges that hadn't had time to collect dust.

One, two...I'm coming for you.

She stood in front of it for a long moment, her blood chilling.

Behind her, Trevor's sharp intake of breath was the only sound he made. Then he was beside her, reading it, and she felt the shift in him — not fear, not for himself. Something more focused and more protective than fear.

"He was in this room while we were in the bedroom," he said.

"Yes."

"Listening."

"Yes."

She thought about that. About Morrison standing on the other side of a wall while she crouched beside a woman he had left alive, hearing her work through his logic, understanding that she was finally inside the design rather than observing its edges. He had carved this and left through the window, knowing she would find it. Knowing what it would feel like to stand in front of it.

"He's trying to get into your head," Trevor said.

"He's been in my head since day one," she said. "That's not new." She turned from the window. "What's new is that he's announcing it. He's not being subtle about my name being last on the list anymore. He's putting it on walls."

Trevor looked at her with an expression she had seen develop over ten days. "This changes the operational picture," he said. "You know that."

"I know."

"You still don't go anywhere without me. Not a scene, not the parking lot, not the bathroom down the hall. That's not negotiable, and I'm not going to let you argue me out of it."

She looked at him. "I wasn't going to argue."

That surprised him. She could see it.

"Good," he said, after a moment.

EMS moved past the doorway toward the bedroom, their gear and their voices filling the space with the productive urgency of people who knew exactly what to do. Shea listened to them work, looked at the carved words on the window frame, and let the full weight of where she was in this sequence settle into her without trying to manage it away.

Eleventh day. Ten victims, one alive by his choice. Her name last. His name second-to-last, and Morrison was still out there, was still moving, was close enough to stand in a room she had been in ten minutes earlier and leave a message specifically for her.

She thought about Linda Graves breathing in the other room. Alive because he had decided she would be. The choice between that and Karen Ellis dead in the evidence room was his, and he needed her to feel the distance between those two outcomes as something he controlled.

"He needs me afraid," she said. Wants her afraid.

Trevor cut her a sharp glance.

"He's been building toward me since the beginning. He left me last because I matter to the design — not just as a target but as an audience. He needs me to understand the full scope of what he built before he finishes it." She turned from the window. "Which means as long as he needs me to understand, he won't move yet. He's not ready."

"And when he's ready?"

She held Trevor's gaze. "We won't give him the chance."

They walked back through the house together, past the words on the living room wall, through the open front door, and into the evening air where the neighborhood continued its ordinary business around the edges of everything that had happened inside one of its houses.

The patrol officers stared at her as she emerged. The EMS team was visible through the bedroom window, working around Linda Graves. The street was quiet.

Shea stood on the porch and looked at the carved words still visible through the open door.

This little piggy went to market.

A market was a transaction. An exchange. Something given for something received.

She thought about what Morrison had been building toward — the design, the sequence, the decade of construction that had led to ten bodies and one woman left alive and her name on a frame in someone else's house.

He thought this was a transaction she didn't understand yet. She was beginning to understand it completely. "Morrison isn't waiting for us to come to him."

Trevor stopped beside her. "You think he's going to make a move."

"I think he already has." She nodded toward the window frame, toward the words she couldn't see from here but didn't need to see. "That wasn't a threat. That was a schedule." She looked at Trevor. "He's telling us when. He's just not telling us where."

"Then we figure out where," Trevor said.

"Yes." Hopefully.

She stepped off the porch and into the evening, and Trevor stayed exactly at her side, as the night settled over Misty Hollow.

She had one name above hers on that list.

She intended to make sure Morrison was the one who ran out of time.

Chapter Fifteen

The call didn't come in clean.

It broke across the radio in fragments with voices overlapping and dispatch struggling to maintain control over a channel that had suddenly acquired too many people trying to say too many things at once.

Multiple victims—

Shots fired, corner of Ash and—

Jurors, repeat, jurors—

Shea dashed for the door before dispatch finished the address. Trevor leaped out of his chair and, reaching for his jacket in the same motion, read her before she said a word. They were in the cruiser and moving inside in forty seconds. Shea pushed the vehicle through the residential streets with both hands on the wheel, her mind running ahead, trying to understand what the fractured radio traffic meant before they arrived and found out.

Three victims. That was what dispatch had finally confirmed when she demanded clarification. Three. Not one, not two — the sequence that had been executing one body per day for eleven days had suddenly compressed, multiple targets in a single location.

"This isn't the same." Trevor braced one hand on the dash.

"No," she said. "But it's still him."

"How can you be sure?"

"Because three jurors in one location isn't random. Nothing about this has been random." She took a corner harder than she should have. "He's accelerating. Something changed."

Trevor looked at her steadily. They both knew what had changed.

Her name on the window frame. *You're next.* The discovery that had moved her from investigator to participant in the span of three carved words. "He's getting tired of playing the game. He wants it to be over."

The scene announced itself before they reached it. Two patrol cars blocked the intersection, a third pulled halfway onto a lawn, officers moving with the quick, careful rhythm of people managing something they didn't fully have their hands around yet. The house sat at the center of it all, front door open, lights on in every room, and something about that blazing ordinary brightness against the night made it worse rather than better.

Shea had the door open before the cruiser fully stopped. "Status," she called, already moving.

An officer turned. "Two confirmed deceased. Third is alive, back room. EMS is with her."

"Inside?"

"Yes, ma'am."

The living room stopped her.

Not because of what was there, but because of what wasn't. No careful positioning. No deliberate arrangement. No nursery rhyme staging was constructed with the patient's attention, which had characterized every scene before this one. What she saw instead was a disturbance — furniture pushed out of alignment, a chair overturned, a lamp on the floor with its shade twisted. The evidence of people who had not simply been subdued but had resisted, had moved, had tried.

Two bodies.

The first lay near the doorway, one arm extended, palm upward, fingers slightly curled. A man, mid-sixties, his face turned to the side. The second was farther in, near the couch, like someone who had fallen mid-movement and not been moved afterward.

These hadn't been arranged. They had simply ended.

Trevor stopped beside her, taking it in. "He didn't stage this."

"Not the way he usually does," she said. "But look at where they are."

He looked. Then understood. "They're contained. Within the room."

"He still controlled the space. He just didn't control the resistance." She moved her eyes across the scene, reading it. "These men fought. That's why it looks different. Not because he lost control, but because they didn't go as easily as the others."

She turned toward the back of the house.

The third victim lay in a smaller room. A study or spare bedroom, the furniture pushed to the edges as if to create space, the overhead light on. EMS crouched over a woman on the floor, their movements quick and specific, the focused urgency of people working against a clock they could feel running down.

"She's fading," one of the medics said without looking up. "BP's dropping."

Shea crouched at the edge of the scene, close enough to be heard without interfering. The woman was small, perhaps seventy, her silver hair spread against the floor, her breathing barely audible. Her eyes were partially open, unfocused, tracking something that wasn't in the room.

"Ma'am," Shea said gently. "Can you hear me?"

Nothing at first. Then the eyes moved — slowly, with effort, finding Shea's face and holding there.

"He said something to you," Shea said. Not a question. An offering. A way in.

The woman's lips moved.

Shea leaned closer.

"He said—" The voice was barely there, a thread of sound. "He said we did exactly what he wanted."

The room went very quiet.

"What did he mean?" Shea asked carefully.

The woman's eyes drifted, then came back. "We didn't fail." A pause, the effort of the next breath taking everything she had. "He said — we did it right."

Then her eyes stilled.

The medic checked, looked up, and said nothing. His expression said it.

Shea didn't move for a moment. She stayed crouched beside the woman, the words sitting inside her, arranging themselves into something she needed to understand before she stood up and moved on.

We did exactly what he wanted. We did it right.

She stood slowly.

Trevor watched her. He had heard every word.

"The jury," she said.

He nodded. "All three of them."

"He told her they didn't fail." She looked at the woman on the floor — at the silver hair, at the stillness that had come so fast. A woman who had sat in a jury box years ago and listened to evidence and arguments and testimony and had reached a verdict in good conscience and had spent however many years afterward believing that the system had failed, that she and her fellow jurors had been deceived, that the outcome of the trial was a wrong she had contributed to.

And Morrison had found her at the end and told her it wasn't. He had told her she had done exactly what he needed her to do.

"He manipulated them through the trial," Shea said. "Shaped the evidence, compromised the prosecution, made sure the outcome he needed was the one they arrived at. And they never knew. They thought they were making a genuine decision." She paused. "And whatever they felt about that verdict afterward, whatever guilt or doubt they carried, he used that too."

Snelling stepped in from the doorway. "The texts."

"The texts," Shea confirmed. *Do you remember the trial? Do you remember what you decided?* Not just reminders. Instruments. He had been pressing on the wound of their uncertainty for weeks before he acted, making sure they understood the weight of what he'd led them to. And then at the end, when it was too late for any of it to matter, he had told this woman the truth. Not to comfort her. To complete the design. To ensure she knew, in her last moment, that she had never had a choice.

The cruelty of it was so specific that it took her breath away for a moment. She walked back through the house, through the living room with its two fallen men and its overturned furniture, and stood in the doorway looking at the shape of the scene.

"He came in with three targets and one location," she said. "He's been working one at a time for eleven days, and tonight he took three at once." She turned to Trevor. "That's not patience running out. That's a schedule compressing."

"Because of the window frame," Trevor said.

"Because of the window frame," she agreed. "*You're next.* He announced the endgame. Which means the distance between where he is and where he's going has collapsed — in his mind, in his timeline. He's not working through a list anymore. He's closing in."

Webster came in from the side room. "We've got the number. You'll want to see it."

She crossed to the wall he was standing near. The number was scratched into the surface, not the clean, deliberate carving of the earlier scenes, but rougher, applied with something sharper and faster. The quality of something done in less time than usual.

Eleven. But the roughness of it told her something the number alone didn't.

"He was interrupted," she said. "Or he interrupted himself. He was moving faster than he normally moves." She studied the marks. "

Snelling crossed her arms. "What does it mean operationally?"

"It means we're running out of space between now and whatever he's decided comes next." Shea turned from the wall. "Pull everything on Morrison's known locations, any property connected to him directly or through the shell company Crale used, any address associated with anyone in his network. Every connection we haven't fully run down yet." She looked at Webster. "Tonight."

"On it," he said, already reaching for his phone.

Snelling followed him toward the door, already talking quietly into her own radio.

Shea stood alone in the room for a moment with the rough number on the wall and the sounds of EMS outside and the specific silence of a house that had held three people an hour ago and now held none.

Trevor appeared in the doorway. He looked at her for a long moment without speaking. "You're putting it together," he said.

"I have it together," she said. "I've had most of it for days. What I didn't have was the shape of the ending." She looked at the number on the wall. "He told the jury they did exactly what he wanted. He left me a message on a window frame. " She paused. "He's ready to finish."

"Then we have to be readier," Trevor said.

She looked at him.

The room they stood in was wrong in every way — the smell, the light, the reason they were there — and he was exactly himself inside it, steady and certain and looking at her with the specific quality of attention that had become something she relied on without having decided to.

"When I'm the last name on that list," she said, "and we get to wherever he's decided this ends—"

"We'll be there first," he said.

"You don't know that."

"No," he agreed. "But I know I'm not going to let him have you."

She held his gaze. "I know."

He crossed the room and stood close enough that when he put his hand against the side of her face, brief and certain, it didn't feel like anything other than what it was. She let herself lean into it for a moment, just that, just the warmth and the steadiness of him.

Then she stepped back. "Let's go find him."

He nodded once.

They walked out of the house together into the night air, the street still busy with officers and the retreating lights of the EMS vehicle, the neighborhood quiet and dark around the edges of all of it.

Eleven victims.

Her name still at the bottom of a list that had almost run out of entries above it.

Morrison knew how this ended. He had known since before it started, had built the ending the same way he had built everything else. With patience and precision and the absolute certainty of someone who had never once doubted that the story was his to tell.

Shea intended to change the last chapter.

She got in the cruiser, and Trevor got in beside her, and the night opened up around them as they drove back toward the station and the board and the name that was second-to-last on a list that was almost finished.

Almost.

Chapter Sixteen

The message came through as Shea stepped out of the briefing room.

Not a call. A text. The same unknown number that had been calling for nearly two weeks, and her pulse spiked before she had fully processed the screen.

Trevor saw her face change. "What is it?"

She looked at the message. *You left your door unlocked.*

Four words. No nursery rhyme. No symbolism wrapped around the meaning to give her distance from it. Just the plain statement of someone who had been inside her home, who wanted her to know it, who had moved from leaving bodies in her yard and names on window frames to something more intimate than either of those things.

Her home. Again. Heidi!

Trevor stepped close and read over her shoulder. "We call it in and go together." .

"Together," she said.

Trevor was already moving. "Together."

They were halfway to her house when the radio fractured.

Officer down — repeat, officer down — unit five requesting immediate backup — west perimeter road—

Shea's hands tightened on the wheel.

Deputy Harris — possible assault — suspect fled on foot — requesting immediate—

Trevor's head turned toward her. "That's not coincidence."

"No." Everything in her wanted to head home and check on her dog. Her job duty said she had to tend to the fallen deputy. One choice. Two directions.

"We split—" Trevor started.

"No." She said it before he finished the word. "That's the point of it. He wants us separated."

Trevor held her gaze for a moment. Then nodded. "Call it in."

She grabbed the radio. "All units, all units — respond to Deputy Harris, west perimeter road, officer down. We are en route to a secondary threat location, will redirect when secured." She put the radio down. "If we split up, he has both of us where he wants us. Together we're slower, and he knows that too, but at least we're not giving him the geometry he's trying to create."

Trevor was quiet for a beat. "You're thinking about this differently than you were a week ago."

"I'm thinking about it the way he thinks about it,"

she said. "That's the only way to get ahead of it."

She drove home. Her house looked untouched.

That was always the first thing, and it never stopped being wrong — the perfectly ordinary exterior, the unchanged facade of a place that was supposed to be her ground and had become something else. No broken windows, no visible disturbance, just the house sitting in the late afternoon light as if nothing had happened in the vicinity of it or inside it.

But he'd said she left her door unlocked. Which meant he'd tried the door. Tested it. Walked through it. "I never leave my door unlocked."

Trevor did a perimeter check while she stood at the base of the porch steps, reading the property, looking for what was different. She had learned to look for what was different. Every scene in this case had taught her something about the gap between how things appeared and what had actually been done to them.

"Perimeter clear," Trevor said, returning to her side. "No visible entry damage on any window or secondary door."

"He didn't need to damage anything," she said. "The door was unlocked." She pushed it open. "Heidi?"

Shea moved through the rooms with Trevor behind her, living room, kitchen, the hallway, each space intact and unremarkable, nothing displaced or taken. The absence of obvious disturbance was the disturbance.

Trevor stopped at the bedroom doorway.

She came up beside him and saw it immediately — on the bed, positioned with the deliberate centering of every other object Morrison had placed in every other scene, a small metal object catching the light. Next to the object, lay Heidi, unconscious, but breathing.

She crossed the room and checked on her fur baby, before picking up the shiny object with gloved hands. "Call, the vet, please. I think he drugged Heidi."

In her hand, she held a shoe buckle. Old, heavy, the kind that belonged to a boot or a formal shoe from decades past. She turned it in her hand, feeling the weight of the metal, the deliberateness of the choice.

"One, two," she said quietly.

Trevor exhaled behind her. "Buckle my shoe."

She set the buckle down and turned to the wall.

It was there. Carved into the paint above the headboard, deeper than the other numbers had been cut, as if more pressure had been applied or more time had been spent:

Twelve. One number left in the sequence that ended with her name.

She stood in front of it for a moment. The countdown had always been there. It was just visible now in a different way, in her own bedroom, above her own bed.

"Trevor."

"I see it."

Her eyes moved to the closet. The door stood

slightly open. Not the way she left it, not the natural settling of an unlatched door. Positioned. An invitation or a threat presented as one.

Trevor moved in front of her without being asked, weapon up, and pulled it open fast. Clear.

But on the back wall of the closet, carved into the drywall with something sharp and applied with force, two words that were different from anything that had come before them:

COUNT FASTER

She read it twice. The patience was ending. Not because he was losing control. Because the design was entering its final phase, and the pace required to complete it was different from the pace at which it had been built.

"He's not losing it," she said.

Trevor turned. "What?"

"He's not escalating out of desperation. This is a scheduled urgency. He's shifting gears because the design requires it now." She looked at the words. "He's telling me to move faster because he needs me moving faster. He needs me reactive."

"So, we slow down," Trevor said.

"We slow down," she confirmed.

Her phone buzzed.

Both of them went still. Same unknown number. She answered. "This is Sheriff Callahan."

No breathing. No pause. Just his voice, and something in it was different from every call before. A directness that had shed the last layer of deliberate distance.

"You chose correctly," he said.

"Staying together."

"Yes."

"You should be asking about your deputy."

Her stomach dropped. "What did you do?"

"He was too close to you," Morrison said. "That couldn't continue. Be glad I didn't take your dog." The line went dead.

She was moving before she had fully processed the call, Trevor half a step behind her with Heidi in his arms, both of them back through the house and out the front door into air that had gone cooler while they were inside. She grabbed the radio as she reached the cruiser.

"Unit status on Deputy Harris — west perimeter road — confirm condition."

Static. Then a different voice, tight with controlled urgency: *Harris is down. Blunt force trauma. Paramedics on scene. He's alive but...Sheriff, it's bad.*

She drove first to the vet, dropping off Heidi with a hurried explanation of what might have happened, then, despite everything in her wanting to stay, she headed to the latest crime scene.

The ambulance was already there when they arrived, its lights washing the roadside in alternating color, the paramedics working with the focused speed of people doing triage on a diminishing window. Harris lay on the ground with two medics over him, a third preparing the stretcher.

Shea was out of the cruiser before Trevor had the vehicle in park. She dropped beside the paramedics, close enough to see Harris's face — pale, eyes at half-mast. A wound at the back of his skull.

Harris had been doing a wellness check on a house three blocks from hers. The proximity wasn't coincidence. Nothing in this case had been coincidence.

"Harris." She kept her voice steady and clear, close enough to his ear. "I'm here. Can you hear me?"

His eyes found her. It took effort.

"He said—" Harris's voice was barely there, a rasp beneath the ambient noise of the roadside and the equipment. His lips moved again. "He said you don't get to have help." His gaze flicked to Trevor. "Watch you back."

The words moved through her like something physical.

Trevor, crouched beside her, went completely still.

"You're getting on that stretcher," she said to Harris. "You hear me? That's an order."

Harris's eyes drifted and then came back. He almost managed something that might have been acknowledgment. Then the medics moved in, and she stepped back, and thirty seconds later the ambulance doors were closed, and the vehicle pulled away, its lights receding down the road. Shea stood on the verge watching it go.

You don't get to have help.

She had heard Morrison's logic clearly enough by now to understand what that meant inside his framework. Help was proximity. Proximity was protection. He was going to remove the people around her. Every person he moved against was another degree of separation between her and the thing he had called help.

Trevor stood beside her. "He's drawing a circle around you."

"It appears that way."

"And tightening it."

"Yes." She looked at the road where Harris had been, at the absence his ambulance had left behind. "He's not just coming for me. He's clearing the path to me. Every person between him and his ending is a variable he needs to eliminate or drive back."

Trevor was quiet for a moment. "Then I'm the last variable."

She looked at him.

"He knows about us. The whole town does. He knows you won't let me step back. Which means I'm the last thing he has to account for before he can get to you." The implication of that settled between them without embellishment.

She thought about the closet wall. *Count faster.* She thought about the buckle on her bed, the number twelve. She thought about a man who had been building toward a specific ending for a decade and was now in its final movements, willing to put a deputy in an ambulance to remove a variable and send a message simultaneously.

"He's going to come for you," she said.

"Probably," Trevor said.

"To get to me."

"That would be the logic."

She looked at him directly. "I'm not going to let that happen."

"Neither am I," he said. "Which is why we don't separate. Not for any reason. Not for another radio call, not for another text, not for anything that pulls us in different directions. Whatever he sets up next…we stay together, and we don't let him split us."

"Agreed."

He looked at her for a moment longer. "He said you don't get to have help. He's wrong."

She held his gaze. "I know."

She turned back toward the road, toward the direction Harris's ambulance had gone, toward the town that held somewhere inside it a man who counted down toward an ending he had been planning for a decade. Twelve victims. Her name last. One number remaining.

The next move was already in motion. She could feel it.

She pulled out her phone and called first the vet, who confirmed that Heidi had been drugged, but would be fine, then the station. "Lock down the Morrison evidence files — physical copies, everything we pulled from Hale's laptop, the notebook, all of it. Nobody in or out of that room without my direct authorization." She paused. "And I want eyes on every entrance to the courthouse. If anything moves there, I want to know before it moves."

"You think he's going back to the courthouse?" Trevor asked when she lowered the phone.

"I think he's going somewhere that matters to the ending," she said. "And I think we have less time than we did an hour ago."

She got in the cruiser.

The number twelve was carved above her bed in her own house.

One left.

Chapter Seventeen

The bridge crossing the river at the foot of the mountain should have felt solid beneath her feet. Instead, it had wobbled as she drove her truck across it.

Shea stood at the midpoint of the span. Bolts loosened at specific intervals. Load-bearing supports weakened in places where stress would be distributed unevenly, built up slowly, and announce itself only when someone was already committed to the middle of the crossing.

Just enough to matter. Not enough to collapse on its own. Another part of the game.

Trevor crouched beside her. "He could've taken this whole thing down," he said.

"Yes."

"But he didn't."

She straightened slowly, her gaze moving along the length of the bridge — the steel stretching out over the narrow river, the water below it quiet and dark, the far bank looking deceptively close. Everything about the structure still looked intact from the outside. That was the point. You would never know standing at either end. You had to be here, in the middle, looking at the thing directly, before it showed you what it was.

"He wanted us here," she said.

Trevor stood. "Then we don't stay."

She almost agreed. The word was right there, and she nearly said it, nearly turned toward the far end, and started walking. But something held her in place — not stubbornness, not the professional pride that sometimes made her slower to retreat than she should be. Something more like instinct. A shift in the quality of the air around them, the way a room changes when someone walks in behind you before you've heard the door.

"Listen," she said.

Trevor went still beside her, and for a moment there was nothing — just the wind off the water and the distant sound of a vehicle on the road above the valley. Then, beneath all of it, a sound that didn't belong. A faint creak, metal under strain, traveling up through the structure from somewhere below them.

Trevor's head turned toward the support beams. "That's not normal."

"No."

The sound came again, sharper this time, a low groan that moved through the deck beneath their feet like a current. Shea felt it in her legs before she heard it with her ears, and that was enough.

"We're getting off this bridge." Trevor's voice dropped to the register he used when there was no room for discussion.

They moved together, fast, but not running yet, because running changes your center of gravity, and the surface was already unstable. Shea thought about all of that even as they covered the first twenty yards back toward the far end. The groan came again, and this time it was accompanied by something else: a sharp, percussive crack from somewhere in the substructure, the sound of metal giving up against forces it could no longer distribute correctly.

Then the deck shifted.

Not a collapse, not a dramatic lurch, but a subtle drop and realignment, maybe two inches, that was enough to break Shea's stride completely. Her foot came down wrong on the tilted surface, and her balance went, and for one terrible half-second, she felt herself go sideways. Trevor's hand closed around her arm.

"Go." He pulled her forward. Heidi barked from inside the truck.

They ran. The far end of the bridge was thirty yards away, then twenty, then the sounds behind them were building into something that didn't leave room for measured steps. Metal protested, bolts released in sequence, and the structural logic of the thing was coming apart.

Shea didn't look back. She didn't need to. She could feel the surface becoming less reliable with every stride, and Trevor's grip on her arm was the most certain thing in her immediate world.

"Almost," he said, the word tight and focused, and then they were off the bridge and onto solid ground, the concrete barrier at the road's edge beside them, and behind them a section of the span dropped away with a sound like tearing, metal crashing into the shallow river below in a single violent collision before the water settled over it and went quiet again.

Shea bent forward, hands on her knees, and pulled air into her lungs. Her heart pounded the way it does when the body has been on full alert and doesn't know yet that the immediate danger has passed.

Trevor didn't pause. He turned back immediately, scanning the damage, his jaw set. "He timed it," he said. "He didn't rig it to collapse the moment we stepped on it. He waited."

She straightened. "He was watching us reach the midpoint."

"That wasn't a message." Trevor turned to look at her directly. "That was a kill attempt."

The word *attempt* was doing real work in that sentence, and they both knew it. This was different from what had come before.

Her phone buzzed against her hip, and they both went still. She pulled it out. Unknown number. The same one. She answered without discussion, because at this point the calls were information, and information was the only currency she had.

"This is Sheriff Callahan."

"London Bridge is coming down," he sang. "You moved too soon."

"You miscalculated," she said.

A pause, longer than his usual ones, which told her something even if she couldn't yet say what. "No." The word was quiet and certain. "I adjusted."

The line went dead.

Trevor was watching her face. "He's watching you."

"Not just me." She lifted her gaze and scanned the tree line on the east side of the road, the long stretch of open ground between the bridge and the first cluster of trees, and the road itself in both directions. Empty. Still. "He's watching us. Both of us. How we move together, how we respond, where we position ourselves. He's been doing it since the farm."

Trevor stepped closer to her. Not subtle about it, not trying to make it look like anything other than what it was. "You don't leave my side."

She met his eyes and felt the argument she might have made at any other point in this case quietly dissolve, because he was right, and because the thing she'd just felt on that bridge, his hand, the immediate certainty of his grip, was still present in her body as a kind of evidence. He'd said the same thing many times during this case, but she didn't mind. "No," she said. "I don't."

The radio on Trevor's belt crackled: *Unit three,*

shots fired, repeat, shots fired, location near your position—

He had his hand on her arm again before the transmission finished, pulling her down hard behind the concrete barrier at the road's edge as the first shot cracked through the air — sharp, and close. The second shot came faster than the first, and Shea heard the impact somewhere behind them, a dull, definitive thud against something solid.

"Tree line — east side." Trevor rose just enough to search before dropping back down. His body was half in front of hers in a way that she noticed and didn't address. "Fifty yards, maybe less."

Another shot. Concrete chipped above the barrier, and dust came down between them. Close enough that the sound arrived with a physical pressure. Heidi's barking increased.

"Stay, girl!" Shea ordered. She didn't need to worry about her dog. She was safer in the truck.

"He's not trying to scare us," Trevor said.

"Not this time." Shea's heartbeat was loud and even. "He's not trying to finish it either."

Trevor looked at her sharply. "It sure looks that way to me."

They moved together along the barrier, low and fast, repositioning while another shot rang out — and then silence, abrupt and complete.

Trevor rose slowly, weapon up, scanning. Nothing moved in the tree line. The wind crossed the open ground between and came back empty.

"Gone," he said.

Shea stood beside him and studied the tree line for a long moment. "He wasn't trying to hit us. He's still playing the game."

"He was firing at us," Trevor said carefully.

"Yes. But look at the pattern." She turned back toward the bridge, the damaged section, the distance they'd covered in the last ten minutes, and then back at the east tree line. "The bridge positions us. We run. He watches how we move under pressure, how we work together, where I go when things accelerate. Then the shots. Close enough to matter, spaced too carefully to be rushed. He's not trying to kill us." She looked at Trevor. "He's mapping us."

Trevor's expression shifted into something harder and quieter than fear. He stepped closer — deliberately, without any pretense that it was anything other than what it was. Shea took a slow breath and looked back at the bridge, the torn edge of the deck, the water below still carrying small pieces of debris toward the bend in the river.

"He's done with the system," she said. "The jury, the trial, the symbolism. He's made his point about the trial's verdict. Whatever comes next isn't about that anymore."

Trevor's voice was low. "Then what's left?"

She looked at him.

"Us," she said. "We're what's left." Her.

The case had shifted beneath them the way the bridge deck had shifted, and they stood on new ground now without having chosen to cross over. Morrison wasn't performing anymore. He had been watching, and measuring, and learning, and whatever he had learned was going to determine what happened next, and it was coming fast.

Chapter Nineteen

They shouldn't have gone back to the station, and Shea knew it the moment they walked through the door. Not because anything was visibly wrong, but because everything looked exactly right, and that was its own kind of warning. Lights on, desks occupied, phones ringing, deputies moving between the bullpen and the break room with the unhurried energy of people working a long shift. Normal in every surface detail. But beneath it, something had shifted. She felt it and knew Trevor felt it too from the way his eyes moved as they crossed the floor — tracking every person, every doorway, every sound, his attention distributed across the room in that quiet, methodical way he had when his instincts were telling him something his mind hadn't yet put into words.

"He's pushing us," he said quietly, falling into step beside her. "Still guiding us to where he wants us to go."

"Yes." She didn't slow. She went straight to the

board, because the board was the only thing that had remained constant through everything that had shifted around it — the photographs and the evidence strings and the names…laid out in a language that didn't allow for the kind of doubt that had been creeping into everything else. She stood in front of it and stared at it the way you look at something you've looked at a hundred times before, trying to find what you missed.

Trevor came up beside her. "Walk me through it again."

She kept her eyes on the board. "He builds structure. People, roles, systems — the jury, the trial, the nursery rhyme sequence. Each victim a position, each scene a correction. He needs the structure because the structure is the argument he's been making." She paused. "But he's done with the argument now."

"Because we're not the jury," Trevor said.

"Because we're not the jury." She swallowed. "Now it's personal. I'm the one who failed to get him convicted."

Her phone buzzed against her hip. She stared at the screen for a moment, then answered. "This is Sheriff Callahan."

Silence — but not empty silence. Underneath it, audible if she pressed the phone close enough: wind, open space, and then the low creak of a door, the sound of a structure settling or being moved through. Her chest tightened in a way that had nothing to do with fear and everything to do with recognition. In the background was the tinny sound of children singing, "One, Two, He's Coming for you. Three, Four, Better Shut the Door."

"Where are you?" she said.

A pause, measured and deliberate. "You know where I am."

The line went dead.

She lowered the phone slowly, her mind racing as she pulled his words apart, testing them against everything she knew. "The old house." .

Trevor frowned. "What house?"

She looked at him. "Jennifer's."

Shea had stood years ago in a different capacity and looked at a different scene that had eventually produced the verdict that Morrison had spent however long since deciding to correct.

"That's exactly where he'd want you," Trevor said.

"I know."

"Isolated. Personal. Loaded with history, he understands better than we do at this point."

"I know."

"And you're still going."

She met his eyes. "I don't have a choice. This has to end."

Something moved across Trevor's expression. Not anger, not quite, but something adjacent to it, the frustration of someone who has watched the person they care about say a particular thing too many times. "You always say that." His voice dropped.

"And I'm always right."

The words came out sharper than she'd intended, and they hung in the air between them with a weight that had nothing to do with the case. Trevor didn't back down, which she'd known he wouldn't. "No, you're not."

She went still. Because he was right, and they both knew he was right, and the fact that she kept reaching for that sentence as though it were a tool when it was actually a habit — the habit of not asking for what she needed because asking felt like a vulnerability she couldn't afford — that was something she hadn't quite looked at directly until this moment.

"If we don't go," she said, "he escalates. More people die. The bridge was the clearest version of that — he moved from symbolic to direct without hesitation, and next time direct won't mean warning shots or structural failure, he times precisely enough for us to survive. Next time, it means someone we care about, or it means something final." She held Trevor's gaze. "So, we go."

Trevor ran a hand through his hair, the gesture rough and quick. "Then we don't go the way he expects. You don't walk in there alone because he told you to. That's not a condition we accept."

She looked at him for a long moment. There was a version of this conversation in which she argued, citing logic about how a visible partner would spook Morrison into disappearing, and retreated into the professional language that had always been the most comfortable distance between herself and the thing she actually felt. She didn't take that version. "Okay."

Trevor blinked. He had clearly prepared for more resistance, and its absence landed visibly. "Okay?"

"No team. He'll see it, and he'll vanish, and we'll lose whatever window this is. But I'm not arguing with you about the other part." She paused. "Just us."

Something settled in Trevor's expression — not quite relief, something quieter and more durable than that. "Just us," he agreed.

The drive out of town felt longer than the distance warranted, the road narrowing as they moved away from the center of Misty Hollow and into the older, less-maintained reaches of the county. Trees pressed closer on both sides until the headlights were illuminating only the immediate stretch of asphalt ahead and the dark shapes of branches on either side. Shea's hands remained steady on the wheel, but her mind moved through the house already — the layout she remembered, the rooms she had walked through years ago, the way memory degrades over time into impressions rather than specifics, which meant she was working with an incomplete map of a place where the details would matter.

"You're already there," Trevor said.

She glanced at him. "What?"

"In your head. You're inside that house already, running scenarios." He wasn't critical about it, just observational, the way he had been watching her think for days. "You need to stay in the car for a few more minutes. Love on Heidi. Ground yourself."

The words pulled her back. She nodded. "Okay."

The house came into view gradually, set back from the road behind a screen of overgrown shrubs that had been allowed to expand well past any original intention. It looked smaller than she remembered, though she knew the scale hadn't changed. It was the weight that had changed, the way the house had occupied her memory over the years, versus the modest, weathered reality of it in the headlights. She parked well short of the drive, killed the engine, and let the silence arrive as she petted her faithful K9.

Neither of them moved immediately. There was something in the quality of the quiet around the house that required a moment — the open front door visible even from this distance, a rectangle of slightly lighter dark against the face of the building.

They got out together and crossed the overgrown yard in silence, moving slowly and deliberately, their footfalls quiet on the soft ground, and when they reached the porch steps Trevor's hand brushed against hers in passing — brief, intentional, the kind of contact that communicates something that complete sentences would take too long to say. Heidi whined and leaned against her leg.

"Ready?" he asked.

"No," she said. "Let's go anyway."

The air inside was different from the outside in a way that wasn't just temperature — it was the air of a space that had been closed and used and closed again, carrying something old underneath the more recent disturbance. Heavy and still, the way houses feel when they have been holding things for a long time without anyone to release them. Shea stepped through the door with Trevor and Heidi close behind her, and then took in the living room in one slow sweep.

Empty of people, but not untouched. Furniture had been moved — not drastically, not overturned or damaged, but repositioned with the same quiet deliberateness that had characterized everything Morrison had done. Specific pieces in specific places, angles adjusted, the room rearranged to match something. A memory, or a record, or a scene from a file she had read. She turned slowly, reading the layout against what she knew.

"He's rebuilding it," she said.

Trevor's voice was careful. "The original scene."

The realization settled through her with a cold, exact quality, because it meant they were standing in a reconstruction. Morrison's version of the crime scene that had produced the verdict he had spent all of this time and all of these deaths responding to. They were inside his argument, physically, in a house that he had prepared for exactly this.

A sound came from deeper in the building. Not loud, not sharp, but a shift, a movement, something settling or being settled. Heidi gave a low woof.

Both of them went still, and then moved, because stillness was a choice they had already made on the bridge and chosen not to make again. They crossed the living room together, Trevor's hand at his weapon, Shea's pulse steady and focused in the way it became when everything narrowed down to the immediate distance between here and whatever was next.

They moved toward the sound as she pulled her weapon.

Toward the center of it.

And this time there was no sense of pursuit, no feeling of running behind something faster than them. Morrison had called her here, had opened the door, had arranged the furniture, and waited. They weren't chasing him anymore.

They had arrived.

Chapter Twenty

The house held its breath, and Shea felt it the moment they moved deeper inside. The walls had absorbed something over the years, and whatever it was, it had not dissipated. She had been in houses like this before, places where violence had happened and been cleaned away but not erased, and they all carried the same quality of attention, as though the rooms themselves had learned to watch.

Trevor stayed close behind her, closer than he'd been at the station or in the car, and he wasn't trying to make it look like anything other than what it was.

The living room opened into the same narrow hallway she remembered from ten years ago — the same worn wood floor with its pattern of fading, the same slight drop in temperature where the hallway turned, enough to raise the skin on her arms. Memory is strange that way, how it stores sensory details that the conscious mind has long since filed away. She hadn't thought about this hallway in years, and now her body recognized it before her mind had finished processing the recognition.

"This is wrong." Trevor's voice was low enough that it wouldn't carry past the two of them.

"I agree." She didn't stop walking, because wrong was the condition Morrison had designed for this room, for this house, for all of it. He had been engineering wrongness since the first body. Stopping because something felt wrong was exactly what he wanted.

They moved through each room slowly, clearing the spaces the way they'd been trained, their steps deliberate and coordinated without needing to discuss it. The kitchen was empty of people but not of intention. A chair had been repositioned at a precise angle, a drawer left open three inches, a glass placed at the exact edge of the counter with the careful placement of someone who understands that objects can be sentences. Nothing had been disturbed carelessly. Everything had been touched with purpose.

"He's walking us through it," Shea said.

"Through what?" Trevor asked, though she could tell from the quality of the question that part of him already knew.

She didn't answer because articulating it would slow her down, and she needed to move, needed to keep the thread of the thing in her hands as they approached the bedroom door, which stood open at the end of the hallway with the particular quality of openness that belongs to doors that have been left that way deliberately rather than simply left.

She stopped just outside it.

Her pulse stayed steady. Trevor moved slightly in front of her, a small shift of his body that she recognized and didn't argue with. He looked at her with an expression that said everything he wasn't saying.

"I'm not going in without you," she said.

He nodded, and they went in.

The room had been reconstructed.

That was the only word for it. Not restored, not cleaned, not simply revisited — reconstructed, with the obsessive accuracy of someone who had been carrying the original in their memory for a long time and had finally had the chance to render it physically. The bed in the same position. The dresser against the same wall. The window with its view of the same overgrown yard. Every element placed with a fidelity to the original that could only come from someone who had been in this room when it looked this way and had never let go of what they saw.

But in the center of the room, where there had been nothing ten years ago, a chair had been placed facing the bed. And in the chair sat Morrison.

He didn't look up immediately. He sat with his hands holding a gun loosely in his lap. He let the silence hold for a moment longer than was comfortable, and then he lifted his head and looked at her. Not at Trevor. At her.

Trevor moved forward immediately. "Don't

move." His weapon was up. His voice carried the hard edge of someone who was done with the measured approach and had arrived at a place of complete clarity about what needed to happen next.

Morrison didn't react. Didn't flinch, didn't shift his hands, didn't do any of the things that people do when a weapon is pointed at them. He simply watched Shea with the attentive, unhurried expression of someone waiting for a conversation they have been anticipating for a long time.

"You came," he said. The same voice from the phone calls — calm, measured, emptied of the kind of emotional coloring that other people's voices carry without their knowledge.

Shea stepped forward, staying beside Trevor rather than past him, close enough to be in the conversation fully. "You knew I would." She gestured with her hand for Heidi to stay back.

"Yes." No hesitation. No doubt. "I'd wanted you to come alone. For you to be the one who arrested me. Just like that night ten years ago."

"You don't always get what you want." She made a motion to Trevor.

"Then you're done." Trevor's words cut across the space between them. "Stand up. Hands where I can see them. This ends now."

Morrison's gaze moved briefly to Trevor and then returned to Shea. Not dismissive, not contemptuous — simply accurate about where the center of this conversation actually was.

"You built all of this," Shea said.

"Yes."

"You killed your wife."

"Yes. You know I did." The words came without resistance, without the defensive shaping that guilt produces in the way people speak about what they've done. Just acknowledgment, the same way a person acknowledges a fact about themselves that they have long since finished being troubled by.

Trevor's jaw tightened. "Then this conversation is over. You're under—"

"She was going to leave you," Shea said, and Morrison's attention sharpened in a way that was almost imperceptible, the microscopic shift of someone whose interest has been correctly engaged. "She was going to expose you, and you knew it." She held his gaze. "But you let it happen. She documented the abuse over a long period of time. And you knew she was doing it."

"Of course, I did."

Trevor's frown deepened. "That doesn't make—"

"You let her," Shea said. "You needed her to."

Morrison looked at her with something that in another person might have been satisfaction, but in him landed as simple recognition. The expression of someone who had been correctly understood after a long time of waiting for that to happen.

"Without the jury," he said, "it meant nothing."

He had needed the trial. He had needed twelve

people to sit in a room and hear the evidence — his wife's documented history of his behavior, laid out carefully, systematically — and decide that it wasn't enough. He had needed them to acquit him. Not because he wanted to go free, but because acquittal was the verdict he required. The system worked exactly as it was designed to work, processing the evidence fairly, reaching the wrong conclusion. That was the material he needed. That was what made everything that came after not just violence but argument.

"You needed them to fail her," Shea said quietly.

Morrison tilted his head slightly, the correction arriving with the precision of someone for whom language matters. "They didn't fail. They did exactly what they were meant to do." He paused. "With exactly the evidence they were given, and all failed to bring a guilty man to justice." He stared at the gun in his hand. "I thought so many times of ridding the world of me, but the child inside, the one buried deep in my core, wanted to play a game. To see whether a failure could be brought right."

The room felt smaller than it had thirty seconds ago. Trevor stepped forward again, his voice harder now, the edge in it no longer sharp so much as absolute. "Enough. You're done talking."

Morrison didn't move, and in his stillness was something more unsettling than resistance — the quality of a person who had already completed everything that needed to be completed and was simply present now, available for whatever comes next, without anxiety about what that might be. This had never been about escape. She had understood that on some level since the bridge, since the phone calls, since the carved number on her porch rail. He had always known how this ended. He had built the ending into the design.

"She saw it," Morrison said, his eyes on Shea. "She almost understood."

"You didn't lose," he continued, and the words landed with a precision that told her they had been prepared, held, saved for this room. "You just stopped."

That part of the sentence was true. She had looked at the Morrison case ten years ago and found it insufficient, had felt the incomplete quality of the evidence and the verdict, and had filed it away because insufficient wasn't the same as wrong, not in any way she could act on. She had stopped. And he had been right that she had stopped, and the fact that he was right about that didn't make him right about anything else, but it sat there in the room between them, and she didn't look away from it.

"Shea." Trevor's voice, steady and close, and she felt herself come back to the room completely, back to the chair and the reconstructed space and the man sitting in it.

She took a breath and let it settle. "You made one mistake." She took one more step forward, and Trevor stayed with her as he had stayed with her through all of it, and she looked at Morrison directly. "You think this ends the way you planned. You think because you've controlled every piece of it, the staging, the sequence, the phone calls, the bridge, this room, that you're still directing it. But you're not." She let that sit for a moment. "You're sitting in a chair in a room with two people who walked in here voluntarily, knowing what this was, because we chose to. That's not your plan working. That's your plan ending."

Something moved across Morrison's face, too fast to name precisely.

Trevor stepped forward then, his voice carrying the full weight of everything that had been building since the farm. "It's over."

And this time Morrison didn't speak. He sat in the chair he had placed in the center of the room he had reconstructed, in the house he had chosen, at the end of the sequence he had built, and he didn't argue because there was nothing left to argue about. The balance had shifted. Not dramatically, not with any of the theatrical reversals that stories often provide, but in the quiet, definitive way that things actually end. He had needed the structure, the jury, the system, the roles. He had spent everything he had building and then dismantling those structures. And now there was no structure left, just a room and three people in it, and two of them had chosen each other.

Shea looked at him for a moment longer. "You didn't create justice," she said. "You created a version of events that required other people's deaths to sustain it." She paused. "That's not a correction. That's a lie that cost people their lives."

The silence that followed was complete and final in a way that the other silences in this case had not been. Those silences had contained him — his breath, his attention, the sense of something coiled and patient waiting for the next movement. This silence was just silence.

Trevor moved forward, and Morrison allowed it, and the thing that had been building since the first body on the fence rail finally, quietly, came to its end.

Chapter Twenty-One

The house didn't feel quiet after Morrison was taken into custody. It felt hollow, the way a room feels in the days after furniture has been cleared out, the walls still carrying the memory of what stood against them. Officers moved through the rooms around her, their voices low and procedural, the sounds of handcuffs and radios and careful footsteps filling the space that Morrison's presence had vacated without quite replacing it.

Shea stood just inside the doorway and let them work around her. Trevor stayed beside her without making a production of it. "You okay?" he asked.

She didn't answer immediately. Her eyes were on the bedroom doorway at the end of the hall, on the chair she could still partially see from here, positioned in the center of the reconstructed room with the careful intentionality of everything else Morrison had done. He had sat in that chair with his hands loose in his lap and looked at her as though the arrival of law enforcement in the space he had prepared was simply the next expected element of a sequence he had designed from the beginning. Even taken into custody, he had managed to make it feel like completion rather than defeat, and that bothered her in a way she was still working through.

"I don't know yet," she said finally. "But at least it's over."

Trevor nodded, and the thing she appreciated most about him in that moment was that he didn't follow it with anything. He just let the answer be what it was.

Outside, the sky had darkened while they were inside, the gray deepening into something heavier, and rain had begun by the time they stepped onto the porch. Light at first, then settling into a steady fall that tapped against the porch boards and the leaves of the overgrown shrubs and the roof of the cruiser idling in the drive.

Shea stopped at the edge of the porch and let it reach her, the cold drops on her face and her hands, the smell of wet earth rising from the yard, letting it wash the stench of Morrison's game from her. Something inside her began, slowly and incompletely, to settle.

Morrison sat in the back of a cruiser at the edge of the drive, his hands cuffed behind him, his posture as composed as it had been in the chair, in the phone calls, in every interaction she'd had with him since this began. She walked toward the car slowly, and Trevor fell into step beside her without being asked, Heidi on her other side, which was the only way she wanted it. Surrounded by the two who would give anything to keep her safe.

The officer standing at the vehicle's post glanced at her. "You want a minute?"

She nodded, and he stepped back to a respectful distance. Morrison glanced up as she approached the window. There was no anger in his face, no fear, none of the emotional register that people typically carry when the thing they have been building toward has finally concluded. Just the same attentive awareness he had brought to everything.

"You understand now," he said. Not a question — a confirmation, offered in the same tone he'd used to say *I adjusted,* and *it's about getting it right*, the tone of someone who has been operating from a fixed point of certainty for so long that other possibilities have ceased to feel real.

Shea held his gaze through the window. "Yes," she said, and the word felt different in her mouth than it had when she'd said it inside the house, standing in front of the reconstructed room, surrounded by his architecture. That yes had been the acknowledgment of someone still inside the thing. This one was from outside it. This twisted man had killed his wife, yet wanted the punishment that went along with the murder.

"You think this ends it," he said.

She considered the question seriously because he

deserved that much. "It ends with you."

He tilted his head slightly, and she recognized the gesture from the room. "Does it?" he asked.

The question was designed to open something. Doubt, or the acknowledgment that systems persist and failures recur, and the conditions that had produced the Morrison verdict would produce others. He wasn't wrong about that. The system wasn't a solved problem. It had failed Jennifer Morrison in ways that were real and documentable, and it would fail others. Shea had known that long before this case and would know it long after. But she also knew something else, something Morrison's entire elaborate construction had failed to account for.

She stepped closer to the window. "You needed control. You built everything around it — the documentation, the trial, the outcome you engineered, the jury you needed to fail her. Every piece of it required you to be the one determining what happened next." She let that sit for a moment. "And then you built this, the sequence, the nursery rhymes, the numbers, this house. Eleven people are dead because you needed the argument to continue." She met his eyes. "But you couldn't control what you didn't account for."

Something moved across his face. A small disruption in the absolute evenness of his expression, a hairline fracture in the surface of his certainty. It was brief. It was almost nothing. But she saw it, and seeing it was sufficient, because it meant that somewhere beneath the architecture of his plan was a person who had not been entirely prepared for this version of the ending.

Trevor stepped slightly forward beside her. "You're done." he said.

Morrison's gaze moved to Trevor, held there for a moment with what might have been genuine appraisal, and then returned to Shea. "It's complete," he said quietly. The distinction between *done* and *complete* — done meaning stopped, complete meaning finished on its own terms — was deliberate, and she heard it and chose not to give it the weight he wanted it to carry. Because he was in handcuffs in the back of a cruiser, and the system he had spent years trying to indict was the system currently processing him, and whatever internal architecture he used to understand that as completion rather than defeat was his to maintain in whatever cell he eventually occupied.

She took a step back from the window and stood in the rain. "Nursery rhymes are for children, Morrison."

The rain had gotten heavier while they talked, soaking through her jacket and into her hair, pooling in the divots of the gravel drive. She didn't move to shield herself from it. There was something about the rain that she needed to be in rather than protected from. The cleansing of it falling on her, the cruiser, and on the overgrown yard and on the farmland beyond, without any interest in what had just happened inside the house.

Trevor's hand found hers. His hand was warm in the rain, and she turned toward him and looked at him the way she hadn't let herself look at him in the middle of all of it, when looking too directly at something meant acknowledging how much you stood to lose.

"You stayed," she said. "As always."

"Wasn't going anywhere," he said, and there was something in the simplicity of it — no elaboration, no caveat, no qualification — that reached the part of her that had been braced against loss for so long that she had stopped noticing the bracing.

The cruiser door shut with a clean, final sound, and Morrison was driven away down the narrow road, the taillights shrinking and then disappearing where the road curved into the trees. No final statement through the glass, no last attempt to reframe or redirect. Just the car, and then just the road, and then just the rain falling on the empty drive.

Shea stood there until the sound of the engine had completely gone, and then she exhaled — a slow, full release of breath that seemed to carry something with it, some compressed thing that had been occupying space in her chest for days.

"You did it," Trevor said quietly.

She shook her head. "We did it."

He didn't argue. He never argued when she was right.

They walked back toward the house together, slower now, the urgency that had governed every movement for days having lifted or at least receded far enough that their steps could find their own pace. At the doorway, Shea paused, as she had paused at every threshold tonight, and looked inside at the room where everything had converged — the chair, the reconstructed space, the place where Morrison had finally run out of structure to hide inside. She let herself feel the full weight of it for a moment: the cost of it, the people whose deaths had produced this ending, the years of Jennifer Morrison's life that had been spent inside a marriage to someone who experienced other people primarily as elements in his own design. She didn't look away from any of it. She just held it for the length of a breath and then turned away.

Trevor stood beside her in the rain, not because she needed protection anymore, but because he had chosen to be there, and she had chosen not to stop him, and that was its own kind of answer to a question neither of them had quite asked aloud yet.

She took a slow breath. Then another. The rain fell with its total indifference; the case was closed; Morrison was gone; and the system had held at a cost she would be accounting for long after this night, but it had held. She stood still for the first time in days, not chasing something, not being pulled toward it. Just standing in the rain beside Trevor and her dog, in the quiet that follows when something that has been in motion for a very long time finally stops.

Trevor pulled her into his arms and rested his

forehead against hers. Neither of them spoke, they just felt.

It was, for now, enough.

Epilogue

The idea had been Trevor's in the end, which was the only reason it had happened.

Left to her own devices, Shea would have taken a week off, slept for two days, repainted the back porch, and called it recovery. Trevor had watched her do it after difficult cases before — the way she filled the space that should have been rest with smaller, manageable tasks, keeping her hands busy while her mind worked through the residue in its own slow, private way. This time, he hadn't let her.

He'd shown up at her door four days after Morrison's arrest with a printed map of the California coast, a highlighted route down Highway 1, and a look that made it clear this was not a discussion he intended to lose. Heidi had been at his feet immediately, her nose working the edge of the map with focused interest, her tail moving in the unhurried way it moved when she approved of something without being certain yet what it was.

"California?" Shea glanced at the map.

"Beach towns. Good food. No jurisdiction." He paused. "Heidi's allowed at most of the stops I picked."

Shea had looked down at her dog, who looked back up at her with the patient, steady attention that had always felt less like a dog waiting and more like a dog who had already decided and was simply giving her time to catch up.

"When do we leave?" Shea said.

They picked up the rental SUV in San Francisco on a Wednesday morning, fog still sitting heavy over the bay, the city half-dissolved in white. Heidi occupied the back seat, her head moving between the two windows as they loaded the bags, tracking every passing pedestrian with interest before apparently deciding none of them required further attention and settling her chin on the center console between the front seats.

Trevor looked at her. "She's going to do that the whole drive."

"Yes," Shea said.

"I don't mind."

"I know you don't."

They took Highway 1 south, the road curling along the coast past Pacifica, and the ocean arrived on their right in stages — glimpses between the hills first, then longer views as the land opened, then the full Pacific stretching west with a scale that was different from knowing intellectually that it was large. Shea had the window down despite the cool breeze, her arm resting on the door, the salt air moving through the car carrying a mineral sharpness that her body had no stored response to, which meant it arrived clean, without triggering anything. That felt like exactly the right thing for this week. She breathed it in and watched the water and, for stretches of several minutes at a time, didn't think about the case at all.

Heidi pressed her nose to the gap at the top of Shea's window, scenting the ocean air , her nostrils working rapidly through whatever complex information the wind was carrying off the water. German Shepherds experienced the world so thoroughly through smell that Shea had always thought of it as a kind of reading — Heidi moving through a space the way a person moves through a library, taking in entire histories from things that registered to human senses as simply air.

"What do you think?" Shea asked her.

Heidi pulled her nose back in and looked at her with an expression of considered satisfaction, then turned back to the window.

Trevor smiled at the road ahead. "She approves."

They stopped first at a beach south of Half Moon Bay, a wide pale crescent with the waves coming in larger than anything landlocked daily life prepared you for, the water a deep gray-green that turned briefly translucent at the curl of each wave before it collapsed into white. The fog had burned off by the time they arrived, leaving the sky a clean, washed blue.

Shea unclipped Heidi's travel lead and switched to the long line she used for open spaces, and Heidi hit the sand and immediately became something slightly different from her working self as she put her nose down and began reading the beach in earnest. Every piece of kelp, every depression left by a previous visitor, every place where the tide had recently receded received its full due. Her ears swiveled independently, tracking sounds Shea couldn't hear, and her tail moved with a continuous, easy rhythm that Shea recognized as Heidi's version of uncomplicated happiness.

They walked the waterline, the three of them, with Heidi ranging forward and back on the long line, occasionally stopping to look at the water with what appeared to be genuine interest when a larger wave came in. The first time the foam reached her paws, she started back, looked at Shea with a mild expression of offense, then reconsidered, stepping forward to sniff the retreating water with the focus of someone who has decided that a thing is worth understanding, even if it was rude.

"She's never seen the ocean," Shea said.

"I also stepped back from the foam the first time." Trevor smiled.

Shea looked at him. "You did not."

"I was seven."

"Still."

He glanced sideways at her. "How are you doing?" The question carried the weight of everything that had preceded it without being heavy about it, the way he had learned to ask things.

She considered it honestly. The beach helped with that — there was something about standing at the edge of something that large that made dishonesty feel beside the point. "Better than I expected to be. The weight's still there. I don't think it goes anywhere, exactly. But it feels like the right size now. Like something I can carry without it pulling me off balance."

Trevor remained quiet for a moment, watching Heidi investigate a particularly compelling piece of driftwood. "That's the most you've said about it since it ended."

"I know." She paused. "I'm working on that."

He nodded once and left it there, which was the right thing to do with it.

Heidi looked up from the driftwood and regarded them both for a moment with her steady, intelligent gaze, as though she had been following the conversation and found the conclusion satisfactory. Then she put her nose back down and moved on to the next thing, which was her way of saying that they should too.

They drove to Big Sur in the afternoon with the windows cracked. The road cut along the cliffs above the water, the turns arriving in a continuous rhythm that required Trevor's full attention and gave Shea and Heidi an uninterrupted opportunity to watch the Pacific from five hundred feet up. The ocean changed color constantly with the depth and the angle of the light — deep navy in the channels, a vivid teal over the shallower shelves, green where the kelp forests grew thick below the surface. Heidi sat upright in the back seat with her ears forward.

Trevor pulled over at a turnout without announcing he was going to, and they got out and stood at the low barrier and looked at the coast stretching in both directions. The road they'd come from disappeared around a cliff to the north, and the road ahead curved south into more of the same impossible scenery. The wind was loud here, coming straight off the water, and it moved through Heidi's fur and pressed her ears back and made her squint slightly in a way that looked almost human. She stood at the barrier beside Shea, leaning slightly against her leg, and looked at the Pacific with what Shea could only describe as respect.

Shea put her hand on Heidi's back, feeling the warmth of her through the thick coat, the steady rise and fall of her breathing. "Good girl," Shea said, quietly enough that it was just between them.

Heidi leaned a fraction more firmly against her leg.

Trevor stood on her other side, and for a while, none of them moved, the three of them at the edge of the continent with the wind off the water and nothing ahead but ocean.

They reached Morro Bay as the sun was setting, the volcanic rock rising from the harbor. Trevor had found them a dog-friendly inn two blocks from the water, rooms with windows that faced west, and a small grassy area in back where Heidi conducted an exhaustive survey of every scent left by previous canine guests, which made Shea smile.

She opened her window and sat in the chair beside it while the light went off the water in slow stages, gold then amber then a deep rose that no photograph would accurately hold. Heidi settled on the floor beside the chair with her head on Shea's foot, the warm weight of her grounding in the way it always was, the comfort of an animal who had decided that where you are is where they should be.

Shea sat with that for a while. The water. The light. The dog's weight on her foot. The sound of Trevor moving around in the next room, the ordinary sounds of someone settling in somewhere new, evidence of his presence in the way that mattered most to her right now, which was simply that it was there.

There was a knock, and she opened the door to find him holding two beers and a paper bag from the fish place down the street that he'd apparently identified while she watched the sunset.

They sat on the small balcony while the last of the light left the water, and Heidi arranged herself across both their feet with the cheerful imposition of a dog who considers this a reasonable use of people. They ate and watched the horizon, and the conversation moved the way it does when the hard thing is behind you, and there's no urgent thing ahead — slowly, about nothing in particular, about the drive tomorrow and what Heidi had made of the ocean foam and whether the rock formation visible from the harbor was actually as old as the sign claimed.

"Santa Barbara tomorrow." Trevor crumpled the top of the paper bag. "Then maybe Carpinteria. There's a beach there that's supposed to be good for dogs."

Heidi lifted her head at the word.

"She knows that word," Shea said.

"She knows a lot of words."

"She knows all of them, I think." Shea looked down at her dog, who watched her with those steady amber eyes that had always seemed to her to contain more patience than any one creature should reasonably possess. "She just chooses which ones to respond to."

Trevor smiled. "Smart."

"Smarter than most people I've arrested."

He laughed, and the sound of it went out over the water and disappeared into the dark. Heidi's tail moved once against the balcony floor, approving.

Shea leaned back and looked at the sky, which had gone the deep, clean blue that exists for only a few minutes between sunset and full dark, the color of something in the middle of becoming something else. The case was behind her. Morrison was in a cell. The people who hadn't come home to their families because of a verdict handed down years ago were still gone, and nothing about this drive changed that. She wasn't trying to make it. But she was here, and Trevor was here, and

Heidi's warm weight was across her feet, and the Pacific was doing what it had been doing long before any of them and would do long after.

She breathed in the salt air and let the rest go.

Below them, the harbor lights came on one by one, reflecting in the water in long, wavering lines. Heidi put her chin back down on Shea's foot, and the night came in soft off the ocean, and for a while, there was nothing required of any of them at all.

226

Dear Reader,

I hope you enjoyed, <u>He's Coming for You</u>, the sequel to <u>The Alphabet Murders</u>. If so, please leave a review. Reviews are a lifeline to authors. I hope you're looking forward to the next book in The Sheriff of Misty Hollow series.

www.cynthiahickey.com
Cynthia Hickey is a multi-published and best-selling author of cozy mysteries and romantic suspense/thrillers. She has taught writing at many conferences and small writing retreats. She and her husband run the publishing press, Winged Publications. They live in Arizona and Arkansas, becoming snowbirds with three dogs. They have ten grandchildren who keep them busy and tell everyone they know that "Nana is a writer."

Connect with me on FaceBook
Twitter
Sign up for my newsletter and receive a free short story
www.cynthiahickey.com

Follow me on Amazon
And Bookbub
Shop my bookstore on my website for better prices and autographed books.

Enjoy other books by Cynthia Hickey

Romantic Suspense and Thrillers

The Sheriff of Misty Hollow
Girls' Weekend Survival
The Threat
Evil Returns
Drowned in Silence
Banner of Death
Christmas Burns
High Stakes
The Alphabet Murders
He's Coming For You

Cowboys of Misty Hollow
Cowboy Jeopardy
Cowboy Peril
Cowboy Hazard
Cowgirl Blaze
Cowboy Uncertainty
Cowboy Christmas Crisis
Cowboy Pitfall
Snowed in For Christmas With a Cowboy

Stay on the Ranch with the whole set

Misty Hollow
Secrets of Misty Hollow
Deceptive Peace
Calm Surface
Lightning Never Strikes Twice
Lethal Inheritance

Bitter Isolation
Say I Don't
Christmas Stalker
Bridge to Safety
When Night Falls
A Place to Hide
Mountain Refuge
Silent Retribution

Stay in Misty Hollow for a while. Get the entire series here!

Secrets of the South
The Lovers' Lane Murders
The Prom Night Hitchhiker
Up in Smoke

The Seven Deadly Sins series
Deadly Pride
Deadly Covet
Deadly Lust
Deadly Glutton
Deadly Envy
Deadly Sloth
Deadly Anger
Get the whole set here

Brothers Steele
Sharp as Steele
Carved in Steele

Forged in Steele
Brothers Steele (All three in one)

The Brothers of Copper Pass
Wyatt's Warrant
Dirk's Defense
Stetson's Secret
Houston's Hope
Dallas's Dare
Seth's Sacrifice
Malcolm's Misunderstanding
The Brothers of Copper Pass Boxed Set

Highland Springs

Murder Live
Say Bye to Mommy
To Breathe Again
Highland Springs Murders (all 3 in one)

Colors of Evil Series

Shades of Crimson
Coral Shadows
Indigo Nightmares
Read the whole set!

The Pretty Must Die Series

Ripped in Red, book 1

Pierced in Pink, book 2
Wounded in White, book 3
Worthy, The Complete Story

Lisa Paxton Mystery Series

Eenie Meenie Miny Mo
Jack Be Nimble
Hickory Dickory Dock
Boxed Set

Hearts of Courage
A Heart of Valor
The Game
Suspicious Minds
After the Storm
Local Betrayal
Hearts of Courage Boxed Set

Overcoming Evil series
Mistaken Assassin
Captured Innocence
Mountain of Fear
Exposure at Sea
A Secret to Die for
Collision Course
Romantic Suspense of 5 books in 1

Wife for Hire – Private Investigators
Saving Sarah

<u>Lesson for Lacey</u>
<u>Mission for Meghan</u>
<u>Long Way for Lainie</u>
<u>Aimed at Amy</u>
<u>Wife for Hire</u> (all five in one)

<u>One Hour (A short story thriller)</u>
<u>One Night (a short story thriller)</u>
<u>One Day</u>
<u>One (the set)</u>

COZY MYSTERIES

Daring Dachshund Mysteries
<u>Off the Leash</u>
<u>A Killer in the Kennel Club</u>

The Tail Waggin' Mysteries
<u>Cat-Eyed Witness</u>
<u>The Dog Who Found a Body</u>
<u>Troublesome Twosome</u>
<u>Four-Legged Suspect</u>
<u>Unwanted Christmas Guest</u>
<u>Wedding Day Cat Burglar</u>
<u>The entire Tail Waggin' Series</u>

Tiny House Mysteries
<u>No Small Caper</u>

Caper Goes Missing
Caper Finds a Clue
Caper's Dark Adventure
A Strange Game for Caper
Caper Steals Christmas
Caper Finds a Treasure
Tiny House Mysteries boxed set

A Hollywood Murder
Killer Pose, book 1
Killer Snapshot, book 2
Shoot to Kill, book 3
Kodak Kill Shot, book 4
To Snap a Killer
Hollywood Murder Mysteries

Shady Acres Mysteries
Beware the Orchids
Path to Nowhere
Poison Foliage
Poinsettia Madness
Deadly Greenhouse Gases
Vine Entrapment
Shady Acres Boxed Set

Nosy Neighbor Series
Anything For A Mystery
A Killer Plot

Skin Care Can Be Murder
Death By Baking
Jogging Is Bad For Your Health
Poison Bubbles
A Good Party Can Kill You
Nosy Neighbor collection

Christmas with Stormi Nelson

The Summer Meadows Series
Fudge-Laced Felonies
Candy-Coated Secrets
Chocolate-Covered Crime
Maui Macadamia Madness
All four novels in one collection

The River Valley Mystery Series
Deadly Neighbors
Advance Notice
The Librarian's Last Chapter
All three novels in one collection

Cozies not part of a series
Coffee, Tea, or Murder
Scones to Die For
Mischief and Mayhem

Time Travel
The Portal

Historical cozy
Hazel's Quest

Historical Romances
Novellas
Runaway Sue
Taming the Sheriff
Sweet Apple Blossom
A Doctor's Agreement
A Lady Maid's Honor
A Touch of Sugar
Love Over Par
Heart of the Emerald
A Sketch of Gold
Her Lonely Heart
Abigail's Proposal
Sophia's Hope
Moira's Quest
Savannah's Trial
Josephine's Dream
A Most Reluctant Bride
Competing Hearts
A Teacher's Heart
Lesson of Love

SERIES
Finding Love the Harvey Girl Way

<u>Cooking With Love</u>
<u>Guiding With Love</u>
<u>Serving With Love</u>
<u>Warring With Love</u>
<u>All 4 in 1</u>

Finding Love in Disaster
<u>The Rancher's Dilemma</u>
<u>The Teacher's Rescue</u>
<u>The Soldier's Redemption</u>

Woman of courage Series

<u>A Love For Delicious</u>
<u>Ruth's Redemption</u>
<u>Charity's Gold Rush</u>
<u>Mountain Redemption</u>
<u>They Call Her Mrs. Sheriff</u>
<u>Woman of Courage series</u>

Short Story Westerns
<u>Flowers of the Desert</u>

Contemporary

Romance in Paradise
<u>Maui Magic</u>
<u>Sunset Kisses</u>
<u>Deep Sea Love</u>

3 in 1

The Red Hat's Club (Contemporary novellas)

Finally
Suddenly
Surprisingly
The Red Hat's Club 3 – in 1

STANDALONES
Finding a Way Home
Service of Love
Hillbilly Cinderella
Unraveling Love
I'd Rather Kiss My Horse

Whisper Sweet Nothings (a Valentine short romance)

Christmas Romances (Contemporary and Historical)
Dear Jillian
Romancing the Fabulous Cooper Brothers
Handcarved Christmas
The Payback Bride
Curtain Calls and Christmas Wishes
Christmas Gold
A Christmas Stamp
Snowflake Kisses
Merry's Secret Santa

<u>Holly's Hope</u>
<u>A Christmas Deception</u>
<u>A Christmas Castle</u>

240

Heads up! Some of the links above are affiliate links. If you decide to buy through them, I may earn a small commission (thank you for supporting my work!). It doesn't change the price for you.